JACK

A SECOND CHANCE MARINE ROMANCE

LISA CARLISLE

LISACARLISLEBOOKS.COM

Jack

Copyright 2020, 2016 Lisa Carlisle

Originally published as Dress Blues in 2017 - expanded for this release

Cover by Book Cover Kingdom

The right of Lisa Carlisle to be identified as author of this Work has been asserted by her in accordance with sections 77 and 78 of the Copyright, Designs and Patents Act 1988.

All rights reserved. No part of this publication may be reproduced, stored in retrieval system, copied in any form or by any means, electronic, mechanical, photocopying, recording or otherwise transmitted without written permission from the publisher. You must not circulate this book in any format.

This book is licensed for your personal enjoyment only. This ebook may not be resold or given away to other people. If you would like to share this book with another person, please do so through your retailer's "lend" function. If you're reading this book and did not purchase it, or it was not purchased for your use only, then please return it and purchase your own copy. Thank you for respecting the hard work of this author.

To obtain permission to excerpt portions of the text, please contact the author at lisacarlislebooks@gmail.com.

All characters in this book are fiction and figments of the author's imagination.

Find out more about the author and upcoming books online at lisacarlislebooks.com, facebook.com/lisacarlisleauthor, or @lisacbooks.

❦ Created with Vellum

JOIN MY VIP READERS LIST!

Don't miss any new releases, giveaways, specials, or freebies!

Access EXCLUSIVE bonus content.

Join the VIP list at *lisacarlislebooks.com* and download *Antonio: A Second Chance Marine Romance for free today!*

Join my Facebook reader group!

ALSO BY LISA CARLISLE

Anchor Me

Meet the DeMarchis brothers and their family in these romances featuring Navy SEALs or Marines!

- *Antonio (a novella available free for subscribers. Sign up at lisacarlislebooks.com)*
- *Angelo*
- *Vince*
- *Matty*
- *Jack*
- *Slade*
- *Mark*

Night Eagle Operations

Military romantic suspense with a supernatural twist

When Darkness Whispers

Salem Supernaturals, Underground Encounters, and the White Mountain Shifters, are connected series. You can start with any of them and do not have to read in any order.

Salem Supernaturals

A witch without magic inherits a house with quirky roommates, and magical sparks fly!

- *Rebel Spell*
- *Hot in Witch City*
- *Dancing with My Elf*
- *Night Wedding*

- *Bite Wedding*
- *Sprite Wedding*

White Mountain Shifters (Howls Romance)

Fated mates and forbidden love. When wolf shifters find their fated mate, the trouble is only just beginning.

- *The Reluctant Wolf and His Fated Mate*
- *The Wolf and His Forbidden Witch*
- *The Alpha and His Enemy Wolf*

Underground Encounters

Steamy paranormal romances set in an underground goth club that attracts vampires, witches, shifters, and gargoyles.

- *Book 0: CURSED (a gargoyle shifter story)*
- *Book 1: SMOLDER (a vampire / firefighter romance)*
- *Book 2: FIRE (a witch / firefighter romance)*
- *Book 3: IGNITE (a feline shifter / rock star romance)*
- *Book 4: BURN (a vampire / shapeshifter rock romance)*
- *Book 5: HEAT (a gargoyle shifter romance)*
- *Book 6: BLAZE (a gargoyle shifter rockstar romance)*
- *Book 7: COMBUST (vampire / witch romances)*
- *Book 8: INFLAME (a gargoyle shifter / witch romance)*
- *Book 9: TORCH (a gargoyle shifter / werewolf romance)*
- *Book 10: SCORCH (an incubus vs succubus demon romance)*

Chateau Seductions

An art colony on a remote New England island lures creative types—and supernatural characters. Steamy paranormal romances.

- *Darkness Rising*
- *Dark Velvet*

- *Dark Muse*
- *Dark Stranger*
- *Dark Pursuit*

Highland Gargoyle

Gargoyle shifters, wolf shifters, and tree witches have divided the Isle of Stone after a great battle 25 years ago. One risk changes it all...

- *Knights of Stone: Mason*
- *Knights of Stone: Lachlan*
- *Knights of Stone: Bryce*
- *Seth: a wolf shifter romance in the series*
- *Knights of Stone: Calum*
- *Knights of Stone: Gavin (coming soon)*

Stone Sentries

Meet your perfect match the night of the super moon — or your perfect match for the night. A cop teams up with a gargoyle shifter when demons attack Boston.

- *Tempted by the Gargoyle*
- *Enticed by the Gargoyle*
- *Captivated by the Gargoyle*

Berkano Vampires

A shared author world with dystopian paranormal romances.

- *Immortal Resistance*

Blood Courtesans

A shared author world with the vampire blood courtesans.

- *Pursued: Mia*

Visit LisaCarlisleBooks.com to learn more!

ABOUT JACK: A SECOND CHANCE MARINE ROMANCE

By Lisa Carlisle

When Vivi Parker volunteers at a fundraiser for a cat shelter, she's stunned to run into Jack Conroy, the one man she couldn't have, but had never forgotten. While they served in the Marines, any relationship between them was off-limits. Years later in Boston, the rules have changed.

But so have they.

CHAPTER 1

VIVI

The royal blue gown swished around Vivi's ankles as she walked down the hotel hallway. She added more swing to her step to make the satin swirl. She'd skipped heels; that might have been a challenge with her leg, but the black shoes she'd chosen had a wedge she could manage.

When was the last time she'd worn anything this fancy?

Not since before she'd enlisted. Ugh, that was sad. The last time she'd been excited about dressing up was for her senior prom. A time when she'd been so naïve about—well, everything. Amazing what a few years in the Marines and a deployment that had ended her military career could do to snap someone out of wide-eyed innocence.

She glanced at herself in a gold-framed mirror. She'd scored a great deal on this dress at a consignment store. A woman from Beacon Hill or Brookline had likely paid a fortune to wear it once before tossing it in the donate pile. Vivi had pinned up her hair with a silver comb, and loose curls framed her face. She even wore makeup, something she didn't bother with when volunteering at the cat shelter, as she often came home messy. Her lips curled into a smile.

"You clean up well, cupcake," a man spoke.

Ryan walked toward her from the open doorway to the ballroom. He was the manager of the Boston Feline Rescue Shelter, where she volunteered twice a week.

"Cupcake?" Vivi raised her eyebrows before cracking a grin.

Few people could get away with calling her that, and Ryan was one of them. Now that she was a civilian, she attempted to relax more. The pressure to prove herself had eased. That part of her life was over, and she was in college now, not on a deployment. She was like everybody else. At least, that's what she told herself, although the evidence on her leg indicated otherwise.

"I almost didn't recognize you all dressed up like a princess," Ryan said with a nod of approval.

"That's because you only see me in clothes that I don't mind getting dirty. My volunteer shirt rarely lacks a fine coating of cat hair." She assessed Ryan in his suit, so different from his every day shorts, T-shirt, and floppy hair, which was now combed back. His beard appeared freshly trimmed. "You don't look half bad yourself." She paused and quipped, "*Cupcake.*"

Ryan laughed and rubbed his hand over his freshly trimmed beard. "I'll take that description—sweet and yummy. Yeah, once a year, I get decked out for this shindig."

Although she'd never seen Ryan outside of the shelter, she couldn't picture him fussing too much about clothes. Not with his laid-back nature.

"I'm excited." Vivi glanced toward the ballroom, but couldn't see much besides champagne-colored walls with electric sconces casting a soft light through the doorway. "It sounds so fancy."

"It's fun. A lot of people will be donating big bucks tonight." Ryan rubbed his index finger against his thumb.

"Sadly, as a college student on limited funds, I won't be one of them."

"That's all right." Ryan put his hand on her lower back and steered her toward the ballroom. "Your time helping out here tonight is just as valuable."

She nodded, glad she could do something of use. The shelter had become her sanctuary since moving to Boston to finish her degree. No matter how stressful her life became, she felt more tranquil after visiting the cats. Forget yoga. Petting a purring ball of fur was the best relaxation technique out there.

As they entered through the open door, the scents of spices made her mouth water. Volunteers moved with haste as they prepped for the evening's gala. They'd set out various items for the silent auction on white cloth-covered tables and arranged trays of appetizers on others.

A few volunteers checked in with Ryan about the tickets, auction process, and other tasks.

After they scurried off, Vivi said, "I might not be the best person to balance trays of food." That might be an issue for her due to the slight limp, a morbid souvenir of her final deployment. The limp wasn't that noticeable, but the scars were. The length of her satin dress covered them tonight. From now on, all her dresses would be long.

"I had something else in mind for you." He raised his index finger and his eyes twinkled with whatever he had planned. "Don't worry. It's easy."

He led her to a table with dozens of photos of cats perched on stands inside mason jars.

"Voila." He waved toward the table. "The Cutest Cat Contest. All you have to do is encourage people to vote by putting a dollar in the jar."

Get people who love cats to vote for cute cats? Nice. She'd scored the easiest gig in the place. "Sounds like fun."

"Voting ends at nine." He gestured around the venue. "Then you're free to wander around, eat, drink, mingle." He brought his gaze back to Vivi. "Which is what I plan to do." He smiled. "Steve is coming later."

Ryan lit up when he mentioned his partner's name. Ah, it must be nice to be in love. Her future might be as an old lady living alone surrounded by cats, but that was fine. Life would be less complicated that way.

JACK

"I can't believe you're dragging me to this," Jack addressed his mom and sister as they walked to his truck. "A cat shelter gala? It's going to be bursting with crazy cat ladies!" he teased and raised his hands palms out.

"Oh, please," his younger sister, Carrie, said with a dismissive wave. "Like it's such a difficult sell? You're a big, tough Marine. A night with a few crazy cat people shouldn't faze you."

"I *live* with a couple of crazy cat people," he replied, eying her and his mom.

He'd been back home living with them and three cats as he looked into options after serving a tour in the Marines. One of the priorities was to get his own place. He loved being back in the States with them, but living with them? That was too much. He'd been on his own for too long.

"This is a chance for us all to get dressed up and do something together as a family," his mom added. "And for the cats."

He couldn't deny his mom anything. Not after all the worrying she'd had to endure during his deployment to Afghanistan. He'd spent the last couple of years in Okinawa, Japan, which wasn't as dangerous, but still on the other side of the world.

"I'm going. Have a suit on and everything." He motioned to the gray suit he'd put on for the event.

His mother beamed and covered her heart. "You look so handsome. My boy is definitely a man."

"I'm twenty-six, Mom. I stopped being a boy a long time ago."

"I'm your mother. No matter how old you are, you'll always—"

"—be my baby," Jack and Carrie completed at the same time.

"We know, we know." Carrie laughed.

Jack drove them in his new Chevy Colorado, his splurge with money he'd saved. Since he'd never owned a vehicle as it wasn't practical during his deployments, this was *his* baby.

They navigated out of the residential neighborhood and onto Storrow Drive. The lights of buildings along the Charles River reflected in the water. They passed the Citgo sign near Fenway Park, a landmark reminding him he was back home. Finally.

He'd counted down the last nine months. Being back should have provided him with some comfort, but something was missing. Since he'd been home, he'd had as much direction as a bat without echolocation. What the hell was he going to do with his life now?

It wasn't time to ruminate, so he shoved away that thought for another time. After he took the exit that led through the city and down near the waterfront, he pulled up to the address—some swanky hotel with valet parking.

"I got it," he told the valet. Turning to his mom and Carrie, he said, "Why don't you get out here, and I'll go park."

"Sir, there's only valet parking available," the valet said.

Who couldn't park their own damn cars? Sure, it was a pain in the ass to find a spot in the city, but come on, they weren't helpless. Parking lots might cost a pirate's ransom, but at least someone wouldn't be touching his things.

"I'll find something," he replied.

"But there's nothing nearby," the valet said. He motioned toward the waterfront.

He was probably right. They were surrounded by high-price condos that likely only had parking reserved for residents.

"Just give him the keys," Carrie insisted.

He shot her a look before he relented and climbed out of his truck. "Take good care of her." He handed over the keys and hesitated before walking toward the entrance with his mom and sister.

"I see that expression, and I know what it means," Carrie said in a knowing tone.

"Oh really, what does it mean?"

"That you're being all judgy. Every time you came home on leave, you'd get that look at some point." She nodded back to his truck as the driver pulled away. "It was the valet parking, wasn't it?"

"Come on." He grinned. "How lazy can people get? Why can't I park my truck in the same spot he's going to park it? I'd take better care of it for damn sure."

"Maybe you can't understand it, big brother, but mom and I have these things on our feet called heels." She pointed to their mom's shoes and then her own. "And we also have these gorgeous, yet constricting dresses to deal with while on said heels, so we don't want to hike to our destination any longer than necessary."

"I was going to drop you off, but all right, I get it," Jack replied. "Don't judge a man before you walk a mile—"

"—in his heels," Carrie added with a lilt.

Jack laughed. They both looked great. He loved seeing his mom dressed up and excited for a night like this. He wouldn't let his hang-ups about people touching his things interfere with a wonderful night out with his family.

"Let's get a drink. If I'm going to spend the night with crazy cat people, I definitely need a drink." He took them both by the arm. "Or maybe four."

VIVI

The gala was going swimmingly. Vivi had sampled the veggies sticks and hummus to keep her going through her shift at the cat contest table and the spicy flavors lingered on her tongue. Soft jazz played in the background.

She chatted with attendees and other volunteers about the cats and smiled whenever someone oohed and aahed over how adorable they were. Everyone seemed to be in a good mood—and so far, a generous one, too, which was great for the cats.

A man stood out from across the ballroom. She froze. It couldn't be him.

Not here. Not now.

It could. And it was.

She blinked. She wasn't fantasizing about this. This was the real, earth-shaking deal.

Her pulse quickened and her feet itched to bolt.

What was wrong with her? Why get so skittish over nothing?

She took a deep breath. On the exhale, she brushed her hands over her dress. After the initial reaction to flee passed, she paused to steal another glance.

Jack was still fine. No, better than fine. In a suit, he didn't appear stuffy at all; more like sinfully delicious. He stood over six feet tall with perfect military bearing. His chiseled face was no longer clean shaven, as she'd always seen him, but with some facial hair. He no longer sported the high and tight Marine haircut and had let his hair grow in. The longer style and facial hair made him even sexier. Ooh, she could run her fingers through the sandy brown strands…

Sure, his date would love that.

Figured he'd be with some gorgeous blonde. Her pink chiffon dress showed off her killer body. In her spiky heels, she was only a few inches shorter than Jack. Ugh, she probably had legs as tall as the Prudential Tower.

Oh no, they were walking in her direction. *Must escape.*

Where to? The ballroom was full of white-covered tables, not escape pods. She couldn't very well duck under one despite the odd urge to do so. And she couldn't abandon her station and run away, reacting like a cat spooked by a cucumber.

Oh great, she'd resorted to cat videos on YouTube to describe her discomfort.

If she turned her head, he might pass by without noticing her.

"Vivi? Vivi Parker?"

She knew that voice. That deep velvet baritone.

There was no escaping now.

CHAPTER 2

VIVI

Jack pronounced Vivi's last name as *Pah-ka,* sounding so damn rough and sexy in his Boston accent. It had never failed to send tremors of heat rushing through her.

She turned in what seemed like slow motion, fighting to keep her expression neutral as the bright lights and champagne colors of the ballroom swirled around her. Her gaze locked with the beautiful blue-green eyes of the man that had consumed her thoughts while she'd been stationed in Okinawa. If she was honest with herself, several times since then. She'd wondered where in the world he'd ended up.

Turned out, it happened to be closer than she'd guessed, and at a place she'd never expect—while she stood next to an arrangement of cat photos.

"Lieutenant Conroy." She forced a pleasant smile to mask her discomfort.

"Just Jack."

He grinned, and she was dazzled. His white teeth. That crinkle at the corners of his eyes. It was truly him.

"I'm surprised to see you here, Vivi. The last time was on an island in the Pacific."

"Small world." What she wouldn't reveal was that after her discharge, Boston had a new appeal for her. It was where Jack was from, which had intrigued her. She grew up a couple of hours north in Portland, Maine. She'd told herself Boston was a way to get a stellar education in a college town, yet be close to her family.

Since she'd moved to his home turf, there was a sliver of a possibility that she'd run into him while he was home on leave at some point. *Hoping* might be the more appropriate description.

But here? Now?

"What are you doing here?" Jack furrowed his brows.

"Helping out." She shifted her weight from one foot to the other.

He raked over her body with a slow, appreciative eye. He'd never seen her dressed up like this. Hell, she'd never even seen herself dressed up like this. At least, she looked good tonight.

Jack showed no sign of noticing her injury, such as a surprised or worried expression. Of course not. Why would he? She was being self-conscious for no reason. He wouldn't see her scars under the long dress or notice her limping while she stood still.

Good, she didn't want to explain the cause of it. *Hated* when people asked about it or worse, seeing that look in their eyes. She could tell when they were speculating about what might have happened. As long as she didn't walk, he wouldn't notice her limp. But Jack was sharp. Nothing would get by him, no matter how much time had passed.

His gaze returned to her eyes. Damn, that appraisal was bold. After all, he was here with a woman at his side. Vivi exchanged a quick glance with the woman, expecting fury or jealousy.

Instead, the woman smiled. "I'm Carrie."

Odd. If Vivi had a man and caught him checking out a woman that way, she couldn't promise she wouldn't make a scene.

"Jack's sister," the woman added in a deliberate tone. The way her eyes darted from Jack to Vivi indicated she suspected something had gone on between them.

"Yes, Carrie, my-uh-sister," Jack stammered.

"Vivi. Nice to meet you." Vivi shook her hand.

"I'm guessing you know each other from Okinawa." Carrie arched a brow. "Unless you were deployed to another island I don't know about?"

Jack turned to his sister in a sort of daze. "Island?"

Carrie laughed. "You okay, Jack? You said you hadn't seen her since you were on an island."

"Oh, yes." Jack shook his head and added, "We did. We met over in Japan."

That was it. No further comments. No explanation about *how* they'd met, *when* they'd met, and *why* they'd lost touch.

Probably because it was better that way...

JACK

Vivi is here? In Boston?

Jack blinked when he first spotted Vivi. It wouldn't be the first time he thought he'd spotted her. Hoped.

Dreamed.

This time, there was no doubt. Even with her head turned, he recognized her. He knew her profile; he'd stolen glances at her countless times in the past and had committed her face to memory. She looked different tonight with her chestnut hair pinned up in a soft style and that dress showing off her knockout body.

It wasn't until after he'd called out her name that he second guessed his action. When she'd turned to him with vivid, wide eyes, signaling fear, his heart had pounded in his ears, drowning out the sound of the music in the ballroom.

His hands turned clammy, and he squeezed his glass of whiskey and soda more tightly.

Approaching her might not have been a good idea.

Too late now. They faced each other and had started a conversation, although he sounded like an idiot, a fact confirmed by his sister's smirk.

"So, Jack." Vivi rearranged jars with cat pictures on the round table beside her, only to put them right back where they started. "You're home on leave?"

She was nervous, too. He read the signs. She was searching for something to do with her hands, while giving her a reason to avoid looking at him.

Not a bad idea. It gave him a chance to regroup without her eyes scrambling his brain, so he could converse like a normal person again. He took a deep breath and focused on their surroundings—the hum of people in small groups chatting and Peggy Lee singing *Fever* over the speaker.

"No. I'm home. Home for good."

She knocked one of the jars over, spilling a few dollar bills from it. While she fumbled to stuff the money back in the jar, he stepped closer to help her. Instead, his hand landed on hers. In that moment, his fingers seemed to ignite, sizzling with the heat from the slightest touch. He hadn't touched her soft skin in so long.

"I got it," she said, placing it shakily back onto the table. She backed into his chest. "Oh, I'm so sorry!"

He placed his hands on her upper arms. "It's okay. I've got you." He breathed in her fragrance—some delicate floral scent.

She stepped to the side and glanced away. "I don't know why I'm so clumsy all of a sudden."

From the corner of his eye, Jack caught Carrie's smile widen.

"I'll let you two catch up," Carrie's tone edged up a notch in a knowing tone. "Coming from a military family, I've heard one too many war stories over the years. Right, Jack?"

"Right." He squared his jaw. His nosy sister would definitely skewer him for details later.

"But first, I need to look at these kitties." Carrie circled the table and examined the photos.

Jack caught Vivi's brilliant amber gaze and swallowed hard. "What do we do now?"

"About?" Her eyes sparkled with wonder.

That look did nothing to help calm his rapid heartbeat. He gestured to the table. "About these jars. Are you the big, bad security detail here?" He winked.

So much for acting neutral. He'd slipped from being unable to speak coherently to flirting. Smooth. How was he supposed to act after all this time?

"Oh." She shook her head and touched her cheek. "Kind of." Her lips curled with a whisper of a smile. "I'm fending off any big, bad wolves that come near these kitties." She tilted her head and studied him with a curious glint in her eye. "But more like convincing people to vote for the cat to be featured on next year's calendar. One dollar per vote. Vote as many times as you wish."

Carrie stuffed a few bills in some jars and then walked away.

"Who's your favorite?" His voice sounded husky and flirtatious, like he was trying to seduce her.

That wouldn't be a bad idea. It would be a fantastic idea, in fact. Before he could censor himself, he pictured some of the things they could do if they were alone. All the things they were forbidden to do when they'd served together.

She spread her arms to her sides. "I'm moderating the table, so I need to remain neutral."

He laughed. "I see. Can't play favorites."

As he scanned the photos, tiny mugshots of kittens, fat cats, tabbies, tuxedos, calicos, and more, he considered the possibilities of anything happening between them now. Things had changed. He was a civilian now, and nobody would care if they got together.

Well, maybe he was jumping eight steps ahead. *Someone might care. She might have a boyfriend.*

Time for him to settle his imagination down and take things more slowly. Besides, he had no idea what was going on in his life. Getting involved with anyone was far from his list of priorities. And getting involved with a woman from his past—even if she was someone he'd never forgotten—would add more complications to all of the uncertainties in his life.

A photo of a black cat with green eyes caught his attention, and he stuffed a twenty in there.

"Stella?" Vivi asked.

"I'm a sucker for black cats. Always so misunderstood, you know?"

She replied with a slow nod. "Maybe because they look so mysterious."

The way she glanced at him made his throat tighten. With that curious look, all he could think about was how she'd look at him in bed. He cleared his throat and forced the image aside. "We had a black cat when I was growing up, named Bam-Bam."

"Bam-Bam?" she repeated.

"We named him Rocky, but he was a master of disaster. We adopted him when I was young, and he was a kitten. After he broke yet another glass, I called him Bam-Bam. The name stuck."

She laughed, a sound that sent warm ripples through his chest. "You must be a cat lover?"

He shrugged. Definitely not one of those crazy cat people. "I don't know about that. My mom and sister are, for sure. Not only did we have five when I was younger, but we fostered pregnant females and tended countless litters of kittens."

She gazed at him with an appreciative glint in her eyes. "I never knew that about you. That's pretty admirable."

His heart thumped quicker. Her thinking positively of him meant something.

He laughed to brush it off. "I didn't have much of a choice. Nor did I have much of one coming here tonight." He gave her a full glance once again, taking in the soft curves of her body. Being alone with her had a tempting appeal. He'd like to see her out of that dress and in his arms. "Now I'm glad I came, since I ran into you."

Her eyes brightened as she glanced away and a hint of a smile teased her lips. "It's good to see you, too, Jack"

When she faced him again, their eyes locked once more. The space between them turned palpable with heat that seemed to swallow all the air. All those things that he couldn't say back then came rushing forth.

The past. It was usually best to keep things back there.

So, he surprised himself when he touched her hand and blurted out, "Vivi, save a dance for me tonight?"

CHAPTER 3

VIVI

As Jack walked away, Vivi stared at his back disappearing into the crowd, ogling him like he was a gelato on a hot summer day. A dance with Jack Conroy. Sparks of anticipation lit her up inside, making her liquefy all the way into her core.

It shouldn't have meant so much. After all, it would just be a dance. Several older couples had already started to dance to a Frank Sinatra song.

But it meant so much more to her than just a dance…

At another ball in another country on the other side of the world, their first dance had been prevented when they'd discovered they had no chance of a relationship.

She exhaled and rubbed her hands down along the satin of her dress.

"What do we have here?" A woman who appeared to be in her fifties who'd applied perfume with a strong squeeze stepped before the table.

"It's a contest to vote for the cutest cats," Vivi replied. "One dollar a vote. You can vote as many times as you like," she encouraged.

While the woman examined the options, Vivi searched for another glimpse of Jack through the crowd. The woman inserted a few dollars and smiled at Vivi before walking away.

"Thanks," Vivi said. "Have a great night."

Within seconds, her mind returned to the forthcoming dance with Jack. Since they were now out of the military, she shouldn't sweat this. But three years of structure and discipline about doing things a certain way had a way of sticking. While she tormented herself in debate, more anxiety twisted its way in. It slammed into her with the impact of a tsunami.

Could she even manage to keep up with him on her injured leg? Her muscles clenched, but she forced herself to breathe through the discomfort of dancing on it for the first time since the accident—and who she'd be dancing with.

After all the physical therapy, she *might* be able to pull off a dance. It would be slow, not some highly choreographed number. Still, she didn't want to be seen as fragile, helpless, or handicapped—especially in front of Jack. She hated the pitiful looks people gave her when they heard what had happened. She was still Vivi, damn it. Her heart still beat, her brain still functioned. It was only her leg preventing her from doing the things she'd once loved.

Like dancing.

But she was still alive. Not like some of the others who hadn't made it back. The familiar shadow of survivor's guilt returned, one that had haunted her since the accident, leaving her short of breath. She didn't want—or deserve—the pity.

She continued to focus on breathing exercises she'd learned to help with stress until the tightness in her chest eased. She glanced at the clock. Only twenty more minutes until the voting ended, and she'd be free to mingle.

And dance with Jack.

Bad idea. Bad, bad idea.

Of course it was. Why get so excited about something this minuscule in the scheme of life? It was a dance with a guy she once knew, that was all. Nothing earth-shattering.

It's nothing to do with him. It's simply testing myself. Another step moving forward with adjusting to my new normal.

Too bad her eyes rebelled against her rationalization. How many times did they scope him out across the crowded ballroom. He met up with his sister and spoke to other guests.

Dollars flew into the jars, raising much needed funds for the shelter. She smiled and thanked voters, but her attention kept drifting to him. He stood a head taller than most of the crowd and held himself with the proud bearing of a military officer. He looked good in a suit. Too damn good to ignore.

Several other women gave him appreciative glances.

Bitches.

What was wrong with her? She had no claim on Jack. He was free to talk to any woman he wanted. Or dance with them. Her stomach tightened into knots.

Jack caught her stare from across the room. Her body froze yet sizzled by that searing connection. Her heart pounded, echoing in her ears.

She thought her leg might be the obstacle in a dance. Maybe it was more than that—something terrifying to consider. What else would describe such a strong emotional response to him after all this time?

Had she ever truly gotten over him?

JACK

While Jack's mother and Carrie introduced him to people at the ball, his gaze often returned to Vivi.

Carrie directed them a few steps away from the latest

conversation where they accepted a bite of basil, tomato, and mozzarella on toothpicks from catering staff.

The combination of flavors mixed with delicious perfection in his mouth.

"You have a thing for her?" Carrie asked.

After he swallowed, he forced a neutral expression. "Why do you say that?"

"You're going to burn a hole right through her blue dress with the way you've been staring at her," she teased with a knowing grin.

Was he that obvious? Clearly so. "I'm surprised to see her here tonight."

"And..." Carrie prodded.

"And nothing. That's it," he declared.

"Bullshit. I was there. I almost got scalded by all the sparks flying between you two. You must have had something going on over in Okinawa."

How the hell could he describe what had happened over there? No way was he going to tell her about his clumsy pursuit of Vivi that might have cost them both, big time. Glancing at his sister, another thought struck. Carrie had often argued with him when he played the big brother role, saying he thought he knew what was best for people and pushed them too hard, regardless of what they wanted. But he was her older brother—of course he'd look out for her. And yes, he did think he knew what was better for her, at least *most* of the time.

Had he made a mistake with Vivi? He didn't know. What he'd said was the right thing for them to do at the time and how he'd felt about that decision were two different beasts. "Doesn't matter. It was years ago." It might as well be a lifetime.

"All right, Jack, if you don't want to tell me, fine." Although her tone was nonchalant, he knew his sister. She was dying to hear the entire story.

Carrie steered him toward their mom, who was speaking

with two guys in suits who were around Jack's age. One stood a few inches shorter and had a beard, and the other was clean-shaven.

"Jack," his mother said when she spotted him. "This is Ryan." She gestured toward the bearded one. "He's the manager for the shelter. And his partner, Steve."

After they shook hands and exchanged greetings, Ryan noted, "I've heard plenty about you from your mom. I don't know what we'd do without her. She's always been a big supporter of the shelter."

Jack knew. He'd seen how his mom had climbed out of that quicksand of grief by finding a purpose. "She loves cats."

"I'm guessing you do, as well," Ryan replied, "Since you've joined us here tonight."

Loved cats? Hell, Jack didn't know about that. He'd grown up surrounded by them; they had been part of his life up until the time he'd gone to college and then into the military when his living situation changed drastically. His formative years included many felines for sure.

He shrugged. "I grew up with them. My mom had us help out at the shelter when we were young."

Carrie and his mom were pulled into a conversation with a couple nearby.

"Thanks for supporting us tonight," Ryan said. "If you're interested, we'd be happy to have you help out, as well, however you can at the shelter."

Steve laughed. "Always trying to recruit new volunteers, Ryan."

Jack scoped out Vivi and caught her eye, a potent exchange that seared him with its intensity. When she broke the gaze, he took her in with a longer perusal.

"Do you know the woman in the blue dress?" he asked Ryan.

Ryan furrowed his brows. "Vivi? Yes, she's one of our volunteers."

"We met in Okinawa a couple of years ago."

"Ah, right. Both Marines." Ryan nodded to himself.

"What do you know about her?" Jack asked.

Ryan ran his hand over his hair. "She's in school. Is pretty private. Keeps to herself."

That was it; Jack wasn't going to let this opportunity slip away and go home with more regret.

"Tell you what, Ryan. If you can arrange for the volunteering to happen with Vivi, sign me up this week."

Ryan sized Jack up with a long appraisal. "Hmm. I think that would be a good idea." He gave Jack a knowing look. "I'd be happy to set you two up—with the, um, *volunteering*."

Steve chuckled. "Oh my. Here we go."

"Be right back, love." With that excited glimmer in his eye, Ryan looked like a cat stalking a bird. "Come on. Let's do this." Ryan addressed Jack and strode toward Vivi.

Now? He wasn't expecting Ryan to act so soon, and he scrambled to move his feet into action. So much for the heads up. He hadn't had time to consider the next step. Essential to any mission was a strategy.

It's not a mission, just a conversation.

Then why was his heart beating like he'd pounded three energy drinks?

"Vivi," Ryan said. "I heard you and Jack met in the service."

Vivi's eyes darted from Ryan to Jack, widening. "Yes." Her tone had a hint of wariness.

"Jack used to help out at the shelter when he was a kid." His expressed turned downright satisfied. "Would you be able to give him a tour this week?"

"Ummm—" She appeared to be stalling, hopefully not coming up with an excuse.

"A scaled-down version of the volunteer orientation," Ryan added.

"I—uh—sure."

JACK

Nice. One point in Jack's favor; he'd found a way to spend some time with Vivi.

"Great," Ryan said. "I'll let you figure out the logistics." He glanced at the clock. "Time's up for voting. Jack, you mind helping us count the votes?"

"I can do that," Jack replied.

He stepped beside Vivi. "Where do you want me to start?"

Ryan glanced at them both, standing only inches apart, and smiled as if pleased with something only he knew. "Right where you are. That's perfect."

They divided up the jars and counted the dollars. Being so close to her was distracting. She smelled so good, that same jasmine scent he remembered. He lost count a couple of times and had to start over.

After all the votes were tallied, Ryan stepped up to a podium and leaned into the mic.

"The featured cat for next year's calendar is—" Ryan paused for effect. "Oh, what a great story this is. I'm sure many of you know this cat's story. She was found nearly frozen during one of Boston's biggest storms last winter. She was in such bad shape, we weren't sure she'd make it."

Many in the crowd were already oohing as if already anticipating the announcement. With the way that Ryan was drawing out the lead-up, Jack wasn't surprised.

"And the winner is—Flurry!" Ryan held up a photo of a gray kitten.

The crowd cheered, including Vivi. He glanced at his mother and sister, who were also clapping with enthusiasm.

Vivi leaned closer to him. "We all have a soft spot for Flurry at the shelter, so this is a happy tale."

"Pun intended?" Jack replied with a quirked brow.

She laughed.

After a few minutes, Ryan made his way back over to the table and addressed them both. "Thanks for your help. Now go and have fun. Eat. Drink. Dance." A flash later, he was pulled into a conversation with other patrons.

Jack glanced at Vivi. From the options Ryan suggested, Jack pushed the most appealing option—the one in which he'd have the chance to hold her in his arms for a few minutes. "So Vivi, how about that dance?"

VIVI

Vivi sucked in a breath as she stared into Jack's eyes. The moment she'd both anticipated and feared was here.

"Sure." She feigned indifference, terrified her pounding heartbeat would give her away.

Jack took her hand and led her through the various groups of people in fancy dress to where other couples were dancing out on the floor. Her hand enclosed in his warm one sent heat traveling through her body. Her heartbeat quickened. How could such as a small gesture like that affect her so?

Forget dancing, it was a wonder she could put one foot in front of the other.

Will you get a hold of yourself? When you met him, you were in the Marines. Not some middle schooler with a crush.

She'd been so lost in her thoughts that she hadn't noticed what was playing, *A Kiss to Build a Dream On,* sung by Louis Armstrong.

Jack turned to her and dropped his hand to her lower back, pulling her toward him. That intimate hold struck her with its underlying sensuality. How different from her neutral reaction from when Ryan had led her into the ballroom with a similar gesture earlier.

Although she yearned to close the remaining space between them, she struggled against that urge. Keeping her expression as neutral as she could manage, she wrapped one arm around him and followed his lead.

He moved with suave precision, guiding her across the dance floor. Despite her worries about not being able to keep up, the way he supported her took the pressure off her injured leg. She moved lightly on her feet, rather than the usual encumbrance on her left leg, like she was dragging an anchor around.

She was dancing. Dancing!

It felt incredible. Beyond that was the closeness of her partner. The heat.

Neither spoke, but energy sizzled between them. It was hard to breathe.

Jack was so achingly close she could barely function. His delicious scent wrapped around her—a clean scent with a faint hint of male musk. If she leaned toward his neck, she could drink it in deeper...

"I remember seeing you in Dress Blues in Okinawa." When he perused her from the head down, his eyes twinkled. "And now you're wearing a blue dress."

She stumbled on hearing those words about that crushing night, but steadied herself, hopefully before he noticed.

"You okay?"

No such luck. "Yes," she stammered. "I haven't worn these shoes in a while. Or danced."

"We were supposed to dance that night. We never had the chance. So, this is long overdue." His tone sounded wistful.

He remembered. She exhaled with a shaky breath. After all, they'd never had a chance to be together. As soon as they'd inched closer, they'd been torn apart.

Memories of the night they'd had to sever ties returned; the ramifications of anything happening between them so clear, how could she ever forget?

They'd first met while she took a history course, almost two years ago, which he'd attended as a guest lecturer. A month after the course had ended, she'd run into him at a rock climbing gym. They'd flirted as they'd crossed paths over the next couple of

Tuesdays and had even partnered to belay each other on some climbs. When he'd brought up the Marine Corps ball, she realized he had no idea she was a Marine. People rarely did and usually assumed she was a serviceman's wife or daughter. She didn't have the telltale hairstyle the men had with that high-and-tight cut. He found out soon enough the night of the ball when he'd see her in uniform. She thought it would be an entertaining surprise.

She was wrong.

Foolish and presumptuous. When they'd spotted each other at the ball, in their Dress Blues uniforms, any chance of a future together was destroyed. He was an officer. She was enlisted.

Forbidden by military rules against fraternization.

How the hell hadn't she known he was an officer?

Pieces started falling together. She'd been stuck working and had been late to the class where he'd likely been introduced. And it wasn't as if they'd addressed each other by rank in a gym off base, where he was Jack and she was Vivi.

The next time they saw each other at the gym, he'd asked if she'd talk with him in private. While they'd walked the beach, they talked all night, about *everything*.

"You know we can't do this," he'd said.

Her shoulders had sagged. It was true, but those words still struck with a sharp pang. "I know."

Despite their words and best intentions, a heat simmered between them. As the moon had brightened overhead, the sensual tension between them grew to an unbearable peak. When he'd finally kissed her under the moonlight, their lips lingered, barely moving as if both were unsure it was real. Fascination exploded into raw passion, turning her into a mass of tingles and raw need.

They'd ended up in the sand, hands all over each other, under each other's clothes. If she hadn't pulled away, breathless, putting the brakes on it, they might have made love right there on the beach. A part of her had regretted doing so ever since. Why did she have to be the good girl and say no when all she'd wanted to do was scream yes, yes, *yes*!

They'd agreed they had to go their separate ways. The temptation was clearly too difficult to resist. She switched up her rock climbing schedule after that to avoid him. Running into him would remind her of how stupid they'd been—and what she could clearly never have.

Yes, she definitely regretted not letting things go any further the night they'd kissed on the beach. Even if they couldn't be together, she would have had that one memory. Not a torturous reminder of what almost happened.

But now, here she was almost two years later, dancing in his arms.

It's just a dance.

"You're right," she replied. "Dress Blues and now a blue dress."

"It's kind of strange." He leaned down and whispered into her ear, a gesture that affected her much more than she wanted to admit. "After all that had happened between us, a part of me thinks we shouldn't be doing this now."

Her heart pounded many hard, steady beats before she replied. "Like someone is going to swoop in and tear us apart." She peered at him. "But here in the real world, this means nothing, right? I mean, we're just two people dancing."

They were now civilians. Those military rules didn't matter. Her mind raced with the possibilities.

"Only a dance," he said.

Then why did she find it so difficult to function?

She forced herself to stop analyzing and enjoy the dance. After all the twists of fate that brought them here, she damn well better. Instead, she focused on all the details of the moment. The warmth where his hands touched her, the closeness of his body, his masculine scent, Louis Armstrong singing about a kiss...

The ceiling flashed before her. She was falling. *Oh blast!*

Jack caught her. "Whoa, you okay?"

She'd tripped on the hem of her dress. Of course, she couldn't be graceful no matter how the dress tried to fool her. She struggled to stand upright, but her dress was pushed up, exposing her scarred legs.

No, no, no.

He noticed the ugly raised scars beneath her pantyhose, that horrible crisscross pattern.

Jack stared at her legs before traveling up to her face. "Shit, Vivi. What happened?"

When they'd rock climbed together, she'd worn shorts and her legs were smooth, not marred with scars. Not horrible and ugly, marking her with a visual reminder that she'd never be the same.

Strong emotions stirred like a tornado, creating a lump in her throat. "Please, no. I need to go."

What an idiot she was to go out there and try to dance like that, acting like she was whole again. Normal. She wasn't. She never would be.

"I'm sorry," Jack said.

"I survived." She bit back tears that pricked at her eyes. She turned and walked away from him. No doubt he'd notice her limp now.

He reached her in no time. "Come on, Viv, let's get a drink."

"It's okay, I'm fine," she managed. *I'm fine.* That had been her go-to line for six months, despite the insomnia and nightmares, flashbacks and panic attacks. If she repeated it like a mantra enough, maybe she actually would be one day.

He stuck close to her as he steered them towards a bar. "I get that you don't want to talk about it."

Talk about it? No, never. She didn't need to vocalize how

damaged she was inside and out. Even though the doctors told her not to use words like damaged as it would only thwart her recovery, it was true. How could it not be?

She'd enlisted while young and naïve, thinking she could better her life and change the world. She'd come home cynical. How wrong she'd been. People had died. Nothing had changed for the better.

Instead, she'd returned home shattered. And she'd been one of the lucky ones. Not everyone in her unit had made it home.

Her skin felt clammy, and her quickened breaths grew audible. She needed to calm the fuck down, not sink into her personal hell of grief and regret.

To drag herself from sinking into a chasm, she pictured herself in her new happy place, surrounded by cats and kittens at the cat shelter. The mental imagery of playful balls of fur helped keep her from sinking into despair.

Vivi forced a smile and faced Jack. "You're right. I don't want to talk about it and ruin the night. It was a wild ride, one I don't wish to relive. Ever."

CHAPTER 4

VIVI

When they reached the line at the bar, Vivi tried not to fidget, but failed, tapping her fingers alongside the seam of her satin dress. She wouldn't push away a little liquid courage right now. Jack hadn't pushed her for more details, but the scars and her limp told a story she didn't want to tell—*something bad had happened.*

When it was finally their turn, she ordered a glass of Pinot Grigio from the bartender. He ordered a whiskey and soda and paid for their drinks. She gripped the stem of her wine glass as if it was a lifeline to keep her from going under water. She sipped her wine and the cool liquid soothed her parched mouth.

She and Jack strolled past tables displaying items up for auction, ranging from gift baskets to gift certificates and all kinds of goodies for cat lovers.

"Look, earphones in the shape of cat ears," he pointed out. "Everyone needs those!"

She laughed, grateful that he lightened the mood. It helped

break the tension after he'd seen her ugly scars. Humor was the best antidote. She'd often used self-deprecation as a way to deal with her new normal. It usually worked, but sometimes it was impossible not to slip into despair. Trying to prevent it was as futile as stopping while jetting down a water slide.

A volunteer with bacon-wrapped scallops passed, and both she and Jack each took a toothpick.

"The food here is good," he noted, "But the tiny portions are killing me."

"Not a fan of little bites?" She bit into her scallop. Mmm, delicious. She silently thanked whoever thought of this combo.

He arched his brows. "I like to eat." He gestured at a table of apps. "There are some killer pot-stickers over there with some kind of peanut sauce. I must have eaten half a dozen already." He rubbed his perfectly flat belly as if he was carrying a baby or a massive beer gut. "I'm happy to take down a dozen more."

"I could eat." Although nerves had wormed through her appetite earlier, that small portion reminded to fill her belly.

Besides, food would give them something to do and provide something to talk about other than the past.

They maneuvered their way through the crowd, many who were dressed for a black-tie affair. They sampled the various appetizers and pointed out good options.

"Try the *spanakopita* and mini quiche," she suggested. "So good. I didn't realize how hungry I was until I started to eat."

"Yes, you need to eat," he insisted with a wag of his index finger. "Don't drink on an empty stomach."

"You sound like my grandmother." Vivi laughed. "Also known as the food pusher. She's always offering food and reminding people to eat."

With a mock affronted expression, Jack put his hand on his chest. "I remind you of your grandmother?" He lowered his hand and grinned. "How about a former officer responsible for those under his watch?"

JACK

"But I'm not under your watch." She raised her brows.

He leaned closer to her. "Oh yes, you are, Vivi." His tone dropped to a rich, sensual tone. "In case you haven't noticed, I've been watching you all night."

Shivers of heat ran through her body. "Fine." She tilted her head. "How about you sound like an officer and a gentleman? Who's always doing the right thing?" A flirtatious undertone carried through her words.

He took a sip of his drink. "I think we both know that's not one-hundred percent true."

The look on his face altered, but she couldn't read it. A little sadness, perhaps some regret?

That night on the beach flashed before her. The sultry heat. The passion they'd barely been able to stifle. She bit her lip and glanced across the ball, down at parquet floor. "We stopped things before it went too far." She brought her gaze back to his.

"And maybe we missed out." His eyes darkened to a fascinating shade of forest green.

Her heartbeat quickened and voice caught in her throat.

He glanced away. "Beef teriyaki." His voice took on a lighter tone as he switched the topic. "Let's get some before they're all gone."

JACK

Jack wasn't sure what he was doing with Vivi, but when she'd brought up the past, he shut down. He could have ruined their careers. He shifted their focus to the perfect distraction—food.

As they walked by the various tables and sampled more apps, he kept the conversation on neutral observations. Still, memories of their star-crossed past in Japan replayed in his head.

When she'd stumbled in late to the history class where he was a guest lecturer, he'd instantly been drawn to her. He figured she was a dependent, someone's daughter or worse, someone's wife. But the way she'd looked at him indicated she was interested in him, *and* she hadn't worn a ring. He hadn't made a move since it was unprofessional, but he'd lucked out running into her at a rock climbing gym. They'd chatted and flirted. They talked about rock climbing and other activities they liked to do, like hiking, biking, and kayaking, and they'd noted their favorite spots to do so.

She was his dream girl, he knew that without a doubt. When he'd worked up the nerve to ask her out, she threw him off guard.

"The Marines have a ball on November tenth..." he began.

She gave him a knowing smile. "I'll be there. Will you?"

Whatever he was about to ask next was lost, swallowed by other thoughts. Why did she already have plans to go? Was she in the military? She'd never mentioned it; only mentioned her classes, so he'd figured she was a full-time student. The worse scenario was that she might already have a date.

Who had beat him to it? Son of a bitch had to be a Marine.

After an endless pause, he replied, "Yes."

Before he could ask any more of his mounting questions, an old comrade of his interrupted.

"Conroy, is that you? Haven't seen you since Kabul."

Vivi turned and walked away. Smiling over her shoulder, she added, "Maybe I'll save a dance for you."

Jack stared after her in confusion. He didn't exactly ask her out as he'd intended, nor found out anything more about her or her connection to the military, but she had promised him a dance.

Sort of.

The Marine Corps ball had turned out to be a disaster. When they'd spoken about it on the beach, it had taken another risky turn. Something about Vivi encouraged him to confide in her. He'd done so in a way he had never done with anyone else.

Everything about her drew him closer. The way the moonlight shone on her dark hair. The reflection of the lights rippling on the ocean danced in her amber eyes, giving them a golden hue. And they'd been alone together for the first time, not in a classroom or gym full of people.

He'd been enraptured by her lips. The need to kiss her had grown all-consuming, one that had left him unable to think of anything else, including all the reasons why he *shouldn't* think about kissing her. The way her eyes had flickered to his lips signaled she might have had the same thing on her mind.

He'd finally yielded to that undeniable sensual energy that pulsed between them, drawing him ever closer. He leaned closer to her and cradled the back of her neck. Her eyes had widened before her eyelids lowered and she softened into his caress.

Near delirious with need, he'd closed the space between them and placed a gentle kiss on her lips. For a moment, he'd hovered there, wondering if it was real. Within an instant, his hesitation had lifted and desire exploded. He'd claimed her with a deep kiss, and she'd responded with the same ferocious need. He ran his hands over her body there on the beach, unable to get enough of touching her.

She'd clutched at him as if she'd never let him go. But then, she'd stopped them.

A crushing, frustrating blow that echoed through him like a sonic boom.

She'd been right, but he'd never wanted anyone more than he wanted her.

But she was off-fucking-limits.

That goddamn rule. So stupid. Okay, not completely. There was a reason that officers and enlisted military personnel didn't socialize. If their daily work never crossed paths, what did it matter?

There were exceptions to the rules, and many couples had made it work, but in the 90s, the military had tightened the regulations, coming down hard on those who'd toed over the line.

Jack would never forget seeing her in her Dress Blues that night. It had shattered every hope of a future with her, even if a part of him had refused to accept it.

And now, almost two years later, seeing her in that blue dress did something that scrambled his brains. The imagery tugged at him as ironic, some amusement played on him by the gods. Yet, it also indicated that things were different now.

But so were they.

She'd been injured, and that raised a plethora of questions. What had happened to her and how did it affect her? Had it ended her military career? An ache spread inside him. She must have gone through hell.

He'd seen too many Marines impacted by injuries, both inside and out. Every time, he wished there was something he could do to alleviate the pain. With Vivi, it would be much more personal. She meant something to him, and he'd never forgotten her.

But he was jumping too far ahead. What if she wasn't interested in him any longer? It had been a long time. Worse, she could be with someone else. His chest tightened. That idea was too brutal to consider.

He glanced at her hands, so dainty with her nails cut short. Most important was the absence of a ring. Still, that didn't mean anything. He'd have to find a way to slip that question in.

"Anyone going to be pissed that I'm stealing your time tonight?" Talk about smooth. He blurted it right out without any lead in.

She'd taken a sip of her wine, but when he asked the oh-so-suave question, she almost choked. "If you're asking if I'm seeing anyone, the answer's no."

He exhaled. If she'd said she was married or engaged, he would have to walk away for good.

She wrapped her hands more tightly around the stem of her glass and appraised him. "You?"

"No."

Their eyes locked, and a potent silence followed.

"Lucky for me." What the hell was wrong with him? Why was he ejaculating things out without thinking first? He could be coming on too strong, too fast.

Vivi raised a brow.

Think. Recover. "I wouldn't want someone getting jealous when you give me a tour of the shelter."

She eyed him with a curious expression. "You have nothing to worry about, Jack."

"When do you want to do it? Tomorrow?" Jeez, could he sound any more eager?

"Tomorrow." She clucked her tongue. Her gaze flickered, as if she was checking her mental calendar—or considering the implications of his question. "I don't usually go in on Sunday mornings, but I'm sure the volunteer on schedule would be happy to sleep in if I cover for him. How about nine?"

"Perfect." Something to look forward to tomorrow.

"Jack, there you are." His mother's voice from behind made him turn. "You disappeared."

He spun to face her and grinned. "Right near the food, Mom. You should have known where to find me."

"True." She chuckled.

"Mom, this is—" How could he describe Vivi? "—an old friend of mine. Vivi."

Vivi's eyebrows twitched at his mention of being friends, but she extended her hand. "It's nice to meet you."

"I'm Elaine. Oh, you're a volunteer as well." His mother glanced at Vivi's name tag. "I haven't seen you there before."

"I'm usually there on Tuesday and Thursday mornings," Vivi said.

"Ah, I like to help with adoptions on Monday nights and sometimes Saturday afternoons."

For the next several minutes, Vivi and his mother chatted

about the shelter, talking about cats and things they'd noticed. While they spoke, he studied Vivi.

Her eyes now held some pain, but in a way it made her more beautiful. What had happened to her to give her those scars? Many variations darted across his mind, from IEDs to a car accident. Whatever it was, it hit him with a pang. She must have suffered a great deal. Maybe one day she'd share what had happened, but he couldn't push it. It was too personal and the scars often cut deep. An urge to wrap her in his arms and take care of her swelled up in him, but he pushed it aside. Not a wise decision to come on so strong.

He had another way to take her back into his arm tonight. "Sorry to interrupt, Mom, but I requested this song, so Vivi and I need to head on back out there." He nodded toward the dance floor. *Home Sweet Home* by Mötley Crüe had begun playing. He reached out to Vivi. "Shall we?"

Her eyes widened. Before she could turn him down, he offered his arm.

After he led her out onto the dance floor again, she faced him. "I don't know about this, Jack."

"Why not?"

"This is a bad idea." Her expression turned troubled. "Considering how clumsy I was last time. I almost fell on my ass."

He didn't blame her for being nervous. "But you didn't."

She clucked her tongue. "That's because you caught me."

He noted, "Ah, we avoided a *cat-astrophy*."

Vivi laughed. "You always had a penchant for bad puns."

He'd often joked during his lectures, making the students groan with laughter.

"You mean clever." He winked at her. "Don't worry, I won't let you fall." He wrapped his arms tightly around her waist to reinforce his point. "It gives me an excuse to hold you tighter."

She put an arm around his shoulder. "Glad to know I'm in good hands."

Jack could think of many other ways he could use his hands on her.

"Old Mötley Crüe?" Vivi arched her brows. "I feel like I'm in some 80s movie."

"What can I say?" he replied. "I love rock, hair bands and all. I heard this song on the radio a few weeks before my discharge and have had an ear worm since."

She tilted her head as she glanced into his eyes. "Pretty apt, since you were on the way home."

He replied with a nod. "Guess that's why it stuck."

He took it slow with small, simple steps until she grew more comfortable with the dance. Her scent wrapped around him. All the while he was aware of how good she felt in his arms again. He wanted to pull her even closer to him, hold her cheek-to-cheek, and sway with her until everyone else disappeared and it was only the two of them there together.

A man could dream.

After they fell into the rhythm, he spun her out and back into his arms, "See? All we need is a little practice to figure out how we work together."

The glint in her eyes as she searched him echoed the question in his head. Did he mean more than just the dance?

CHAPTER 5

VIVI

*V*ivi arrived at the cat shelter early the next morning. The familiar odor of cats and cat litter hit her first. It would soon pass after she cleaned out the boxes. She turned on the lights.

Meows followed as the cats trotted to her from all directions in the free roaming shelter, looking to her for food. She greeted the closest ones with playful rubs and maneuvered through the furry crowd to reach their food bowls.

After all the cats were distracted by their breakfast, she glanced at the clock. Jack should arrive soon.

She hated to admit how much she'd been looking forward to seeing him today. The shock of seeing him last night, followed by the overwhelming experience of dancing with him, wrapped in his strong, masculine embrace, had left her too excited to sleep.

A part of her had reawakened when they'd danced. Damn, it had felt good to feel desire again, and be desired in return, something she feared might no longer happen in her post-incident world. He'd seen the ugliness of her scars but had still appeared interested in her.

When she fell asleep, he'd played a reoccurring role in some sordid dreams.

Exciting and somehow terrifying.

Take a step back and rein yourself in. Getting your hopes up over something that has crushed you in the past isn't wise, especially since you've both changed.

Jack strode into the cat shelter and all reason drifted away. Her eyes glued on him, and her throat turned parched. He wore jeans and an olive green T-shirt clung to his chest and biceps. She snapped her mouth shut before she drooled His arrival in her sanctuary did things to her body that left her unable to function.

How would she focus on what she was supposed to do? The sensual pull between them last night had been almost too much to bear. They'd be alone, not surrounded by dozens of people in a ballroom. Well, alone, save for the cats. And the felines wouldn't give a rat's ass—or, would it be cat's ass?

Wait, what was she thinking?

Jack met her gaze and greeted her with a lopsided smile. Combined with that striking twinkle in his eyes, the effect was panty-melting. She dropped what was in her hand.

Oh hell, it was a cat litter scoop. She was caught scooping poop. How devastatingly alluring. She put it in its storage container and went to greet him before washing her hands.

She wiped any jaw-dropping remnants of awe off her face, shooting for a neutral expression. "You made it."

Despite her step down from the blue satin cocktail dress the night before to her current appearance—gray yoga pants, the standard orange volunteer shirt, and casual ponytail, he gave her an appreciative glance. "Wouldn't miss it, Vivi."

That penetrating look, the deep huskiness in his voice as he said her name in that incredible accent…

God, he made her body react with such volatility. Her insides shot into motion like he'd set off illegal fireworks in an off-limits area. She suppressed a snort. That was the impact he'd had on her since they'd first met.

She needed to get herself in check. Do what she was tasked with, which was get him up to speed on volunteering at the shelter. She'd done the same for at least a dozen people before, no big deal. Give him the tour, show him the ropes, point out some of the cats' quirks, and that would be it.

Vivi drew in a shallow breath and exhaled through her nose. In a detached tone, she said, "You mind signing in there, Jack." She pointed to the volunteer sign-in sheet. "And when you come in, wash your hands here."

She needed to wash hers as well so stepped into the gated enclosure for storing cleaning and grooming supplies and closed the gate behind her. To the cats, it would be another area to explore—and wreck. Too many things were in there they shouldn't get their little paws into. She lathered up in the sink. After she rinsed, she stepped back to reach for a towel when she bumped into something hard.

His chest.

That hard, tantalizing chest she'd been so close to last night.

Vivi gasped. "Oh! I didn't know you were in here."

She turned to him, and it put them face to face in that confined space. Had it always been so small in there? Her breath came out in quick pants. Her attempt to remain professional melted under his penetrating gaze.

"Sorry. Didn't mean to startle you." His voice came out a low, sensual croon.

Without the wedge heels she wore last night, he loomed over her. He was like a life force, drawing everything to him. And she was the closest object to get caught by his gravitational pull.

Damn, his eyes sparkled, like an ocean shade between blue and green under the fluorescent lights. Those weren't flattering for most people, but for him, they accentuated that captivating blend of colors under his dark lashes.

And his lips—so defined, so kissable. They were right there. If she leaned up on her tiptoes…

Don't go there…

"I guess I didn't hear you open the gate over the sound of the running water." Why was she talking so fast? Was it because her heartbeat was pounding so fast around him?

His mouth spread into a decadent smile, as if he knew exactly what she'd been thinking about his lips. "Now that you have me, what do you want to do with me?"

All those fantasies from last night flooded her brain and a wave of heat rose in her cheeks. For a Marine who'd faced combat situations and countless come-ons from the men she'd served with, she should be able to handle an easy training like this. But something about Jack made her revert to the awkwardness of a high school freshman with a crush on an unattainable rock star.

Her lips parted as she attempted to find a suitable answer. "Um, what do you mean?"

He chuckled. "I still need to wash my hands, but then what?"

Oh, dear God, he meant at the shelter, *not* what she'd been envisioning he could do with those sensual lips.

"Let me get out of your way." As she tried to slide by him, her breast rubbed across his arm. Bad move. What was she, one of the cats rubbing up a person's leg for attention?

Or maybe marking her territory?

If her cheeks had simmered with heat before, they'd blown up into a full-blown inferno now. She slipped out of the gated area without brushing up against him with any more accidental seductive moves.

He's only a guy you once knew. He's only a guy you once knew.

And kissed...

With the disarming effect he had on her, maybe this wasn't such a good idea after all.

JACK

Volunteering at the shelter had turned out to be a great idea. Jack had been there less than ten minutes and already found his body pressed against Vivi in that enclosed space.

Sure, it had been accidental, but hey, he'd take any excuse to touch her. He'd wanted to since the first moment he'd seen her in that classroom. It had been an intensive summer course on US history, made more intense with her presence in his class.

Last night, when they'd danced, he'd kept a respectable amount of space between them, despite his body urging him to pull her closer. It was torment having her so close, but unable to touch her in all the ways he wanted.

A moment ago—a highly charged moment—he thought they'd kiss. It took all his willpower not to bend down and go for it while she looked up at him with eyes wide and lips parted. But he couldn't take her and kiss her senseless in the middle of the cat shelter, even though it seemed like a damn good idea.

But hell, when her breast rubbed against his arm, he tried not to moan in pleasure like some goddamn frotteur on the train. If he affected her, just a fraction of how she affected him, they'd be lucky to get out of there today without going at it against the fence.

What was wrong with him? He was reacting to her like a horny teenager hit by a mass of hormones.

Once Vivi left the gated enclosure, he forced himself to get in check. After all, he was in there to wash his hands, not to take her right there, cupping her ass as he lifted her off the ground surrounded by supplies for cat care. Hardly a romantic setting.

Focus. Stop getting distracted by things that will most definitely not be happening right now.

"This is the main area," she said, bringing him back to the matter at hand. As they walked, she pointed out the large room filled with cat trees, toys, and litter boxes. "You've been here before, right?"

Memories from when he'd visited with his mom when he was younger returned. "It's been a long time. Some things look familiar, but at the same time, a lot has changed."

Vivi tilted her head. "It's kind of cute seeing you here."

"Why?"

"You know, seeing a big, tough Marine around cute, furry cats." She smiled.

"Says another Marine doing the same thing."

"Well, people—" Her gaze drifted off as she appeared to search for the word.

"Suck?" he offered.

She laughed. "I wasn't going to say that, but yes, sometimes they do."

"My sister has a T-shirt with that printed on it," he explained. "And that's why you spend your time here, I guess."

She shrugged. "Perhaps. I've always loved cats."

Volunteering here had to be her escape, her sanctuary, the same as it had been for his mother. She'd pointed out the numerous physical and mental benefits of pets, such as reducing stress.

"Do you have any pets at home?" he asked Vivi.

"No." Her smile disappeared. "Tough to find a place to rent that allows four-legged tenants, and rents are high enough as it is."

"True." Boston's real estate prices could be brutal. "I'm in a housing search myself."

"Looking long?" she asked.

The way she peered at him made his pulse zigzag.

He rolled his shoulders back, forcing his mind on the question. "I've only been back about six weeks. Living at home with my mom and sis and four felines. In other words, desperate to get out of there."

She laughed again. He loved that sound and loved it even more that he was the one that made her happy.

"Did you have any cats in your house growing up?" he asked.

"Unfortunately not." She frowned. "My mom is allergic. Once I enlisted, it wasn't like I could have one with me in the barracks or on deployments."

Vivi pointed to a dry erase board on the wall with photos of the cats and notes on their care. "This chart is key. You can see if they're on a special diet or medication, or even their likes and dislikes. Volunteers update it every day. The early birds like me give them food and meds. I'm guessing you'd help more with socializing. Check these notes first and add any quirks you find for others."

After he scanned the info on the board, noting some of the names and key points, they moved on through the main room, while cats eyed them with wariness from their perches.

"Did your mom drag you to the ball last night?" She asked. "And convince you to come here today?"

"Affirmative to the first question. Negative to the second one."

She arched her brows with a skeptical expression as she appraised him. "You decided to volunteer on your own?"

"Of course. It gave me an opportunity to spend more time with you."

He'd had to pull away from her back when they served in Japan, but circumstances had changed. And he was a man, not a monk.

Vivi stopped mid-step and faced him.

When he caught her beautiful eyes, he swallowed hard. He might be pushing it with coming on too strong, but why not take a chance? They were denied it in the past. He'd be a fool to miss the opportunity now.

"Back then, we did the right thing. But I never stopped thinking about you." He resumed the pace while holding his breath. When a fluffy black cat with green eyes rubbed up against his leg, he was grateful for the reprieve in the heightened tension.

A black cat crossing his path. A sign of good luck or bad?

Good, definitely good. Black cats were misunderstood, getting an undeserved bad rep. He bent down and opened his hand, letting it come to him and sniff before he rubbed its chin.

"That's Stella," Vivi said.

She hadn't replied to his admission of thinking about her. He retreated, following her lead to focus on the cats. His mom volunteered for a reason. It brought her purpose, some sort of happiness after his father had died. Had Vivi found something here after what had happened with her leg?

"I think she's the one I voted for last night," Jack noted.

"That's right," Vivi replied. "If you sit down, she'll climb on your lap. She has no shame."

He laughed and sat his ass on the tile. As Vivi said, Stella crawled right onto his lap. He rubbed her cheek and under her chin. "You just want a little attention is all, isn't that right?"

Stella stared at him with her big green eyes, nudging his hand when he took a break.

He resumed the cheek rubs. "She's a sweetheart."

"Careful." Vivi raised her index finger and grinned. "Or I'll be filling out the adoption papers soon."

"Ha, I barely know what I'm doing with my own life right now, let alone being able to commit to taking care of someone else." He stroked her soft fur, and she purred. "She's so friendly. I can't believe she's not adopted already."

When he glanced at Vivi, the corners of her mouth turned down and a furrow mark appeared between her brows.

"She's eight. She came here after her owner passed away last year." Her tone lowered with concern. "It's harder to adopt them out when they're older. Everyone wants kittens. Sometimes they don't realize how much work they are and bring them back. Many of them would be better off adopting an older cat."

While he stared at her, admiring how much she cared for the animals, Stella jumped off his lap. She sauntered off with her tail in the air. He raised his hands to the side and addressed Stella with mock offense. "Was it something I said? Did I rub you the wrong way?"

Vivi laughed. "Cats are funny that way. They take what they want until they don't want it anymore."

That was one option. Cats would be cats. "Or I scared her off." Searching her face, he followed up with a loaded question. "Am I scaring you off, too?" He'd been careful not to come on too strong, try to balance his advances with some humor, but it was difficult to restrain himself around her.

Vivi pursed her lips. "That's not it. Trust me, I was very excited to see you last night, but now I wonder…" She shifted from one foot to the other. "So much time has passed, Jack. I'm not even the same person you met back in Okinawa. I was so foolish. And now…"

When she didn't finish the sentence, he prodded her for more. "And now, what?"

She closed her eyes and reopened them. "I shouldn't be with anyone." She took in a deep breath and exhaled. "I know I'm not supposed to say what I'm about to, but it's true."

He paused, waiting and fearing what she would say next. "Say what?"

She lowered her glanced across the room. "I'm broken."

His chest tightened. Her admission was exactly what he feared. Many service members had come home changed, or shattered in one way or another, including him. A disturbing memory wiggled loose from its shackles, rising up into his mind. The confusion, the helplessness, the guilt.

He shoved it back down. This wasn't time to feel sorry for himself.

Seeing that lost look on her face tugged at him in a way nothing else had before. Vivi, once so vibrant, now suffering.

"No, I don't believe it," he said in a gentle tone. "You're still *you*."

She gestured at her leg. "I'm twenty-two, but sometimes my leg gets so stiff, I move like I'm eighty."

He took a step closer to her and brushed his fingers against her hand. "Sure, your physical abilities may have changed, but you are still the same amazing person you have always been. You have the same heart and the same core. Sometimes it takes time to remember that, but those important things don't change."

She raised her gaze to meet his. "It's easy for you to say. You're whole. Not marred by a flash that changed your life in an instant. And it's more than just physical repercussions—there's insomnia, nightmares, anxiety…"

It was all a mask. If she saw inside his head, she'd see how lost he was, confused. Wandering about, haunted by ghosts.

Raw pain flickered in her eyes. He guessed she didn't talk to many people about this. But they'd found a way to connect back in Japan and cut through the bullshit.

"What caused it?" he asked.

She crossed her arms and gazed off. When she didn't answer right away, he figured she wouldn't at all. But in a low voice, she said, "Roadside bomb."

An ache swelled in his chest. All he wanted to do was take her in his arms and brush away any of her pain.

"I'm sorry." What else should he say? What else *could* he say? "That must have been—tough."

She busied herself by retrieving a grooming brush and bent

over to scoop up a calico cat with a mat on its side. "Come here, you," she said to the cat. "I know you hate this, but you're terrible at getting them out yourself."

Was this a deliberate tactic to steer the conversation away?

While she brushed the squirming cat in her arms, she said, "And yet, what right do I have to complain? At least, I made it home alive, right?"

The cat clawed her and jumped to freedom, running away.

"You okay?" he asked.

"Oh well, got most of it," she said. "I'll find her later."

He swallowed a lump that welled in his throat. "Want to talk about it?"

Vivi swallowed. "Not much more to tell. I'm sure you've heard similar stories. I was deployed to Afghanistan, where we were hit and lost two of our own. Many of us were wounded. After months of rehab, I'm doing better."

"Glad to hear that," he said. "The emotional toll is sometimes harder than the physical one."

Vivi closed her eyes and nodded, but the pain remained visible on her face. When she reopened them, she asked, "Did you ever face anything like that?"

Her question instantly dragged him back to the desert. All the sand, the uncertainty. The gunfire. The precious blood spilling out of Martin's opened chest. And the fear—the crushing inevitability that they wouldn't be able to save him. His heartbeat fired up and breath came in fast.

"Not quite like that." He squared his jaw, attempting to rein in his body's reactions. *One-two-three.* He counted to eleven before he could squash the memories back down where they belonged—buried. He wiped his hands on his pants, hoping she would leave it at that.

Her gaze dropped to his hands and then raised back to his eyes. "We should get back to work."

He exhaled. She must have sensed his unwillingness to talk about that experience.

That conversation was over—for now. His heartbeat slowed to its normal pace. He focused on the reason he was here.

"Got it." He glanced around the room. "What else do you want to show me?"

She eyed a litter box that appeared to be recently used and arched a brow. "Are you above scooping poop?"

An unexpected laugh escaped him. "I spent years in the Marines, Viv. Dealing with shit every day was an unwritten part of the job description."

The smile she gave him made his heartbeat fire at a rapid tempo. He'd deal with a hell of a lot worse than cat crap if it meant he could make her beam at him like that once more.

CHAPTER 6

VIVI

*B*reathe.

Vivi's rib cage tightened around her lungs, piercing her like splinters. The familiar anxiety had returned when she told Jack about how she was injured.

She hated thinking about that moment, dreaded reliving it. But uttering those few words here—in her protected space—to someone who'd faced similar situations was easier than in the past, when she'd quickly shut down. He'd faced his own demons. She'd caught a glimpse of the pain in his eyes. She'd recognized the signs of discomfort and didn't push him to talk about it.

When she'd confided in Jack, she hadn't said much. But for her, those few words describing the incident were monumental.

And most of all, he'd made her smile.

She took a slow, deep breath to alleviate the claustrophobic sensation and exhaled. Fortunately, one of the next stops on the tour was outdoors.

Her breathing returned to normal as she returned to her volunteer mode and finished showing him where the cleaning supplies were and what volunteers could do to help out.

"This is the courtyard." As they stepped outside, she inhaled the scents of the trees. She motioned to the large fenced in space that gave the cats plenty of outdoor areas to explore, but kept them away from the danger of cars, predators, and other threats. The leaves had begun to change, and the trees surrounding them draped the enclosed space with the colors of sunset. "Not much for us to do out here except for occasional clean ups, some light landscaping, or separating aggressive cats."

Jack turned as he scanned the area. "Easy enough."

She raised an eyebrow. "Clearly you haven't wrangled apart two territorial felines."

He leaned closer to her. "Perhaps you'll have to show me how to do that." His voice came out with a smoky, almost teasing tone.

His fingertips brushed her hand, making her keenly aware of him. Was it accidental? When he did it again and lingered, the answer was clear. If it was any other man, she might have pulled her hand away. As it was Jack, she didn't dare move.

One heartbeat pounded. Then another. "I think you can handle just about anything, Jack."

He entangled his fingers with hers, a warm and somewhat intimate move that left her spellbound. The way he stared at her with such heat left her skin tingling.

She was caught in his eyes, that soulful gaze. She lost all sense of time as he seemed to see right through her, reading her every guarded thought, especially those that centered on him.

"Anything?" he replied. "Not likely." His voice was pure decadence now. "Especially when I'm distracted, like now."

Desire pooled low in her belly. It took her a moment to find her voice. "By what?"

The heat in his stare was scalding. Her heart pounded in her ears.

"I was thinking about the time we kissed in Okinawa." He brushed a strand of hair that had slipped from her ponytail off her cheek, and his fingers lingered before he pulled it away. "Our one and only."

Her breath came quicker. She was practically panting. "It was—a good kiss."

That was how she responded? A good kiss? Try a freakin' awesome kiss, one she'd replayed countless times since then. Forget about the dozens of fantasies where she rewrote their ending on the beach. And those times, she didn't kill the happy ending.

"It doesn't have to be just one." He cupped her chin and brushed her bottom lip with his thumb. "Or only." He dropped his hand, leaving her suddenly bereft and missing his warmth.

God, his vitality strummed at her every nerve, leaving her breathless with longing.

He stared at her lips and swallowed.

The waiting was torture. Torture! Her skin burned like it was covered with cinders, yet she still yearned for his touch. If she didn't have his lips on hers in one more second…

Screw it. She leaned up to him and bridged the gap to kiss him, aware that she'd never initiated before. Every guy she'd dated had pounced at the earliest opportunity, and it had been up to her to control the pace. But Jack had drawn out her anticipation until she'd been on the verge of climbing the walls.

Her first step in taking control of what she wanted—it was bloody amazing. Exhilarating. Fueling her with some sort of powerful delirium that spurred her to continue.

Jack froze at first, but then spurred into action. He held the back of her neck like a predator, refusing to let her escape, and claimed her mouth as his.

After all the time that had passed, one thought zipped

through her. Oh, hell yes. She was still a woman. She still felt. She still had needs. Maybe she wasn't completely wrecked as she had feared.

Most of all, she was finally kissing Jack again. God help her, she would not put the brakes on this time. She wrapped her arms around him, holding on to him as if refusing to let him go.

His tongue slipped in, swirling around her own, as she lost sense of everything else. Kissing wasn't foreign to her. She'd been kissed many times, but nothing ever felt like this. Perhaps it was the buildup, perhaps it was from wanting him for so long.

Or perhaps it was because this was Jack freakin' Conroy, and she'd never wanted anyone the way she burned for him. He'd been forbidden and yet so decadently tempting.

His fingers slid over the side of her neck, trailing her shoulder, before reaching her breast. She could scarcely breathe, arching toward him, begging him for more. How her body responded that quickly surprised her.

Many thoughts volleyed in her head, but they were drowned out by her body's rising desires. When he stroked over her nipple with his thumb, a strangled noise escaped her. Yes, she wanted this. Needed him.

Needed more.

The slam of a door jolted her. He pulled away from her, leaving her in a daze. What was going on? Where were they?

The familiar scene of the outdoor courtyard brought her back to reality with the sight of a few cats napping under the autumn sun. Shit, they were making out at the cat shelter. It must have been Ryan entering the front office.

She smoothed her clothes, wondering if her outsides matched her scrambled insides.

Jack raised his hand. "Your hair."

He ran his fingers through some unruly strands that had slipped from the elastic. She couldn't walk into the office looking like she'd had a quick shag in the courtyard—which she might have ended up doing if the door shutting hadn't shattered the spell. And hell, it wasn't like the cats would give a crap.

Still, it was unprofessional. They weren't two teens looking for a quick hookup. She pulled her hair out of her ponytail and smoothed it back into a tighter one. She took a deep breath to focus. "Thanks."

"You okay, Viv?"

He'd snapped back upright, but the way he jutted out his jaw indicated he might be as flustered—and frustrated—as she was.

"Fine," she managed to respond. "I better go check in with Ryan, let him know we're here."

"I'll wait out here." He gave her a devastating grin that made her mind fuzzy again. "I don't think he'll want to see me until my Jolly Roger lowers its sails."

She laughed and lowered her gaze. Hot damn, his erection was visible, straining against his black jeans. Resisting biting her lip at the promise bundled in that decadent package before her, she forced herself to put one foot in front of the other to walk to the office.

JACK

Jack prowled over the lawn in the courtyard, still wound up by the kiss. He wasn't ready to talk to anyone. How could he converse when all he wanted was to touch Vivi's lips again?

A few cats sized him up from under the cover of bushes like they'd been trained in the military to seek cover. They were likely assessing the stranger—him—and gauging if he was a threat. Others napped as if oblivious to his presence.

He bent down and extended his hand to present himself as friend, not foe. A brave orange tabby strolled over and sniffed at his fingers, but once Jack rubbed its cheek, it turned and scurried back to its hideaway under foliage.

Jack rose and resumed pacing the lawn. He wanted to get out

of there and take Vivi some place private. Somewhere he could take her in his arms, tear off her clothes, touch her and kiss her everywhere…

Control yourself. Just because you haven't been with a woman in a long time doesn't mean you have to go all caveman on her.

He grunted. Part of the reason was he hadn't met anyone whom he'd clicked with since Vivi. No one gave him any tingles, no one set off any sparks the way she had. And conversations, forget it. They were the worst part. Each time he went on a date with a woman, talk was forced, not at all natural.

With Vivi, their discussions had that underlying passion right away. They'd started in class when they'd debated topics ranging from historical to current events, evolved through their flirtation at the gym, and then exploded during that intense all-night talk on the beach. They'd only known each other a short time, but had cut through the bullshit right from the start. In a world full of fakes, that meant something.

Something to treasure.

Jack's memories returned to one in particular, when he'd teased her about his absolute belief in the existence of Big Foot and how he'd gone on hunts to find one. She'd insisted that all the so-called "footage" was fake. He loved riling her up as she often responded with a passionate reaction. She'd skewered him with questions until he broke out into a laugh. That was what he remembered most about her—not only could they talk, but they could laugh.

The problem was, after he'd met Vivi, he didn't want anyone else but her. Even knowing he couldn't have her.

But now, they might have a chance—if he didn't blow it. He couldn't barge his way into the cat shelter and take her like some beast, despite all the primal urges driving him to kiss her again. To touch her soft skin. To taste every secret part of her. To push himself inch by inch inside her, making her gasp, and cry out his name.

Running into Vivi again gave them a second chance. What he knew was that he wanted her in his life. It might be crazy to think that way, but after many years in dangerous situations, he listened to his gut.

And his gut told him not to let her go.

A black cat sauntered out from the cat door. It was Stella. She strutted over to him like a disinterested princess, but then rubbed his leg with vigor.

"Hey, sweet thing. Coming out for some fresh air?" He bent down and opened his palm.

After she sniffed it, he rubbed her cheek. That only encouraged her to push for more, and she nudged his hand when his efforts slowed or weren't vigorous enough.

"Damn, you know exactly what you want, don't you?" He laughed. "It reminds me of someone else." When Vivi had initiated the kiss, it had thrown him off balance in an oddly exciting way. He thought he'd been the one leading the seduction, but when she'd taken the lead, he'd almost lost control.

If the kiss had been that hot, he couldn't imagine what it would be like to bury himself deep inside her.

Oh yes, he could. He'd done so already, dozens if not hundreds of times.

If she was on board, it was time to make his fantasies come true.

Vivi walked back into the courtyard. His breath caught in his throat. She was stunning.

"Look who's back." She nodded at Stella.

Jack swallowed. "I think we're going to be best buds before I leave."

Vivi planted her hands on her hips and grinned. "I might get jealous."

"You don't strike me as the jealous type."

She shrugged. "I don't like to share."

His gaze raked over her. If he had her, he wouldn't share her with anyone. It would take all his self-control not to tear into any man who coveted her. Now that he'd kissed her again, his inner alpha had already claimed her as his, even if she didn't know it yet.

He stepped closer to Vivi. "Who does?"

Another searing gaze passed between them again, hot enough to incinerate the whole damn building. It would be a miracle if he made it out of there today without taking her on the soft earth in the courtyard, rolling her over the crunchy fallen leaves.

"Anyway, let's get back to work." Vivi motioned ahead. "Let me show you where some other cats are. They've tested positive for Feline Immunodeficiency Virus, and need some extra love."

Jack couldn't keep his gaze from wandering over her during the next hour as she finished the tour with the other rooms in the building, introducing him to more cats.

Focus on her instructions. Not fantasizing what else you could be doing with her.

After countless times catching him ogling her, she called him out on it. "You keep staring at me."

"You're very stare-able."

She burst out with a laugh. "That's a new word."

He arched a brow. "One that would make Shakespeare proud?"

She shook her head, though her teasing smile lingered. "I'd stick with history if I were you."

CHAPTER 7

VIVI

*A*fter that kiss, it had taken Vivi several moments to return to the present. She'd felt weightless over the next hour, floating like a drifting cloud as she and Jack finished up at the cat shelter.

They ended in the office to check out with Ryan. He spun in his office chair to face them and assessed both with an amused glance. What was he smirking about? He hadn't seen anything, had he?

Unless her feelings were clearly scrawled across her face. That kiss had ignited something within, leaving her with a burning she wasn't sure she could extinguish.

Her attraction to Jack had taken another turn in their sensual dance, moving closer and pulling back, leaving her scrambling to find a steady foothold. After all this time, would they finally have a chance to start something new?

"You all set, Jack?" Ryan asked.

"Think so. I had an excellent orientation." Jack grinned at Vivi.

"Stella took a liking to him," she burst out at a higher pitch than usual. Talking about the cats would be safer.

"The feeling was mutual," Jack agreed with a nod.

When she'd seen Jack playing with Stella, it had tugged all the more at Vivi's already well-worn heartstrings. Everything about him seemed to be designed to break down her barriers and barrel through her reinforcements like an armored vehicle, leaving her exposed and vulnerable.

Perhaps talking about the cats wasn't so safe after all. Or maybe it was all Jack. She inhaled to steel herself and focus on her tasks, doing a quick mental run down to make sure she hadn't missed anything.

After they said their farewells to Ryan and exited the office, she pulled her hair out of the ponytail and it fell over her shoulders. Jack leaned against the exterior of the main building and hooked his thumbs through his belt loops while he watched her.

His gaze traveled over her. "What are you doing the rest of the day?"

That look suggested all the decadent things they could do, and her brain hummed with a sensual static. She shifted her feet through the pebbles in the parking lot. "I have a couple of classes this afternoon."

"What time?"

"The first one starts at two."

"What classes?"

She twisted her hair into a knot and teased, "You ask a lot of questions."

He took a step away from the wall and closer to her. "I'm interested in learning more about you, Vivi."

Her heart stuttered a pleasant heat simmered in her veins. "Okay then, one is animal biology, the other is on the history of Boston. I'm majoring in animal science with a minor in history."

"Odd combination. But history, good choice." The sparkle in his eyes was following by a conspiratorial wink.

She raised a brow. "I once met a lecturer in Okinawa who sparked my interest."

Whoa, that was super flirty. A memory of his lectures returned. He'd spoken with such conviction about the material he'd presented that he'd commanded everyone's attention. She never caught anyone dozing off.

That had been a long time ago. Time to get over that. But that dance last night had set everything in motion once again, launching her anticipation to new heights. To tame her excited nerves, which clambered like an untamed filly, she added, "An interest in history, of course."

His smoldering gaze appeared bluer under the bright skies without a cloud in them, and they scorched her as he drank her in. How could he affect her so with just a look?

He took another step closer to her and traced his fingers down her forearm, lingering on the back of her hand before he pulled it away. "How did you end up enlisting, anyway? What drew you to it?"

Her heart beat so loud that it echoed in her ears. She shifted focus to his question and not the desire coiling deep in her core. "Not really sure. I graduated high school and wasn't ready for college because I didn't know what I wanted to do with my life. The military seemed like a good option." Her words tumbled at a rapid pace that matched her quickened breath. "I could learn about myself, see the world, and take some college classes." She pointed at her leg. "I was a teenager and thought I was invincible. Guess I was wrong."

His eyes warmed with concern. "We all think that way when we're that young. And we can't anticipate stuff outside of our control."

She shrugged as she scanned the area. The shelter was between brick apartment buildings off the main road in a more residential neighborhood of the city. "So now I'm here, using the GI Bill, and trying to get my degree. I'm hoping to work with animals, however I can. The history minor is more of a personal interest."

"Sounds like you have a good plan." When her gaze returned to him, his intense eyes were still on her. "Maybe you can offer me some tips about getting my life in check after the military. How about over dinner tonight?"

Vivi's muscles tensed. His question left her unbalanced. That time they'd made plans to meet at the ball, it had ended up a monumental, crushing disaster.

She inhaled and squeezed some of the tension out with the exhale. Nothing was stopping them now, right? Nobody's career would be threatened. They were finally free to do what they wanted.

Then why did she feel as if she was tempting fate by going back for round two?

What was it about Jack that affected her so? He shouldn't elicit such a strong reaction in her. Almost two years had gone by. She'd moved around, faced all kinds of challenges, and had now started the next phase of her life.

But his dark, steady gaze did things to her that defied explanation, making her think whatever connection they once had was as raw and consuming as ever. Not to mention the kiss. That would get her through many cold, lonely nights in the near future.

She glanced down at the asphalt of the road. It stretched ahead and veered off to a tight curve, an unexpected adjustment if driving too fast. One moment could change everything.

The attraction wasn't the problem. It was her. No matter what progress she made, she feared she'd lost her spark. It had burned out with the fires that had marred her flesh and ended her military career.

JACK

Jack waited for her answer. Despite all the reservations in her head, every part of her body responded otherwise.

Over the jumble of static in her mind, she forced out her reply. "Sure."

He rewarded her with a magnificent grin. "I'll be looking forward to it all day, Viv."

After Vivi went to class that afternoon, she found a seat in the back of the lecture hall. She barely took in the professor's words as she thought about Jack. Fortunately, this class was in a larger auditorium and not one of the smaller discussion groups where she'd be expected to participate.

How could she focus when she had a date with Jack that night? How could she not think of how they'd kissed in the cat shelter that morning? How could she not fantasize about seeing him again?

Anticipation drove her to check the clock every few minutes.

When her classes were finally done for the day, she rushed from campus back to her apartment. She took a long, hot shower, and visualized Jack in there with her. Those intense eyes capturing her as he touched her and whispered dirty things in her ear. She lingered too long and had to rush to dry off and find something to wear.

After fishing through her closet, she chose a long-sleeve orange and brown patterned dress that was fitted up top, but flared out from her waist. The flattering design echoed the colors of fall in New England. Luckily, boots were in style. She could wear a dress with leggings and her scars wouldn't be visible.

As she applied light makeup, her excitement at the night ahead stared back in her expression.

Settle down. Don't hype this night up and set yourself up for disappointment. Remember what happened last time?

How could she forget?

She played classical music to help calm her while she finished getting ready.

Thirty minutes later, she stepped off a Green Line trolley to meet Jack outside a tapas restaurant. The sun was lower in the sky above the buildings along the city skyline. The cooler evening air felt welcome as her body had seemed to burn at a higher temperature all day.

He paced in front of a commercial stretch of brick buildings, looking as handsome as hell in a blue button-down shirt and black pants.

Despite that buzz of anticipation that had fueled her all afternoon, a strange calm fell over her as she headed over to him. Being near him again made everything right again.

When he spotted her, his gaze caressed her. He leaned forward and kissed her cheek. "You look beautiful, as always."

Tingles of delight danced through her. "You look pretty good yourself, Jack."

He took her hand and led her to the entrance. "I'm glad you came tonight."

"Me, too."

JACK

Each time Jack saw Vivi, he fell for her a bit more. She was this enticing combination of strong and sexy. Seeing this side of her in a perfectly fitted dress made his brain signals misfire, most of which redirected straight to his groin. All he'd been able to think about since they'd kissed was continuing where they'd left off.

Tonight, he wouldn't let her go without making his intentions known—he wanted her. In his life, in his bed.

He wanted her. Simple as that.

Whether she'd go for it or shoot him down was the question.

They entered the restaurant, a family-owned one tucked into a modest brick building in a commercial stretch. He loved establishments like this, the mom-and-pop businesses rather than the massive franchises. It made him feel like he was supporting a family rather than a corporation.

They walked by dark wooden walls with low lights that focused on the bright Spanish paintings. Exotic spices scented the air, making him salivate.

Their server led them to a tiny table with a white rose and a tealite candle. They ordered a pitcher of red sangria and tapas, choosing various plates that the server recommended. After their drinks and tapas sat between them, they sampled each one. The delicious flavors of warm cheeses, spicy meats, and seafood lingered on his tongue.

He drank some sangria and glanced at her. "It's funny that you ended up here in Boston. And we ran into each other in the most unlikely of places." He couldn't believe his luck when it came to crossing paths with Vivi again.

"Ending up in Boston isn't that farfetched." She shrugged. "Maine is only a couple of hours away."

"You once told me you thought you'd go to school around here." He covered his chest and teased, "Here I was hoping that you moving here had something to do with me."

When she tensed, he thought he'd hit close to her reason.

"I thought you were over on the other side of the world." She raised a brow and followed with a saucy look. "I don't remember you being so cocky."

He laughed. "Perhaps a little hopeful that you're as happy to see me as I am to see you."

"Maybe." Glancing away, she sipped her sangria before returning her gaze to him. "What did you do today?"

"Not much. My mom had me help move some boxes in the

basement. Now that I'm back, she's putting me to good use with plenty of home projects."

"You're a good son." She tossed her shiny brown hair over her shoulder and gave him a teasing grin. "I'm glad you didn't say you went out looking for Big Foot or something like that."

He chuckled, remembering the shared moment in Okinawa. "That's on the agenda for tomorrow." He winked.

Their conversation turned back to Okinawa, which led to a question he'd heard dozens of times: "How did you end up in the Marines?"

He eyed her before he replied. Funny how they hadn't talked about that until now, another quirk in their strange and bumpy road that led him to the present.

Should he tell her the real story or the quick version to shut everyone up? Yes, he could trust her. She'd get it.

He wrapped both hands around his glass. "My dad was a Marine. He died in Afghanistan when I was twelve."

Vivi sighed. "I'm so sorry."

"Since it was just Mom and Carrie, I took on the role as man of the house, following in his lead. I went to college nearby so I could take care of them and joined ROTC. There was much I didn't know about my dad. By learning more about the military, I thought I'd learn more about him. Naturally, my mom was worried about me considering a military career, but she understood—I was trying to be like my dad. When I graduated, she told me to do what I wanted to do. And off I went."

She'd leaned in closer as he told the story, lips parted as she listened intently. "I'm guessing you didn't want to make a career out of it?"

He took a sip before answering as he considered what had become clearer to him during the end of his tour in the Marines. "True. What I found is that it wasn't a lifelong career for me. I'm more fascinated about military history than living a military life. It gave me more insight to my dad—and maybe myself."

"What did you discover?" Her interest sounded genuine.

He tapped his fingers on his thigh as he sought the right words. "Something was missing while I served. That's why I started teaching over there. And once I started to do so, something clicked. It was what I wanted to do." He took one of the cheese tapas off of a colorful plate and chewed.

Vivi's eyes were still fixed on him. "And now that you're home?"

The million dollar question. After he swallowed, he replied. "I'm wondering the same thing. I've been trying to figure out my next step."

She raised both hands palms up. "It seems obvious to me. Why don't you teach?"

How much more should he reveal? He didn't know her *that* well to tell her his secrets.

Her eyes were full of interest as she waited for him to answer. It was rare that anyone looked at another like that, invested in the other person. Most people, he found, barely listened. They waited for the break in the conversation so they could talk once again.

"I'm not sure I'm cut out for it," he admitted and fixed his eyes on the table before raising them back to her.

Vivi shook her head and looked at him from under raised brows. "Come again?"

"I'm serious."

"Jack, I was in your class. If anyone was cut out for it, it's *you*."

He shifted in the chair. "It's different here."

She watched him. Clearly, she wasn't going to let it go with such a vague answer.

"We live in a university mecca here with brilliant people all around us," he explained. "Harvard, MIT, BU, BC, the list goes on. It was one thing to lecture at an extension school overseas, but it's another to try to land a teaching position here. I'll need to take more classes."

He left one part out, that small fear that nagged at him. *I don't know if I'm good enough to run with this crowd.*

"But you have what it takes, Jack."

Vivi said it with such conviction that he straightened in his chair. He took a sip of sangria, which turned out to be more of a gulp.

Her eyes were bright as she gestured with her hands. "You have that enthusiasm, no—*passion*—that inspires others."

He shrugged and poked at a piece of chicken, moving it around the sauce on the plate before shoving it into his mouth. It was tasty, like the rest of the meal, but he barely took notice, not when they had moved their dance so perilously close to his deep, dark insecurities.

After he swallowed, he went one step further. "Some of my cousins are veterans and they gave me a heads up about the rough transition back to civilian life, but I have to admit, it's been harder than I expected."

Seconds passed. She didn't seem to blink.

"I know *exactly* what that feels like."

She understood, and that encouraged him to continue. "But it shouldn't be as difficult for me, right?" Now that he'd opened the jar of concerns, they flew to the surface. "I don't have any injuries to hamper me. I should just get over it and move on. But still." He ran one hand through his hair. "Something's off. It's like I'm drifting. Lost at sea." He motioned with an open hand. "It's what many of us dream about—to come home and start a new life with our loved ones." He shook his head as he squared his jaw. "And now I'm home, but everything's different."

"It's us, I think," Vivi replied. "The world hasn't changed. We have."

"My cousins, Angelo and Matty, describe it like trying to fit a puzzle piece that has been reshaped by water back into position. It might fit, but it will never be seamless."

She made a sound of acknowledgment. "That sounds about right to me."

Her words played in his head as they finished their meals. After they exited the restaurant, they lingered in the parking lot, exchanging glances. She seemed as unwilling to leave as he was, shifting her feet, but not making any motion to leave.

"Let me drive you home," he suggested.

"You sure about that? The Green Line is right here." She motioned to the tracks cutting down the center of the road. "And parking can be tough in my neighborhood."

"It's a small price to spend more time with you." He reached his hand out to touch her cheek and stroked her soft skin.

She leaned into his hand. "Then let's go." The decadent glimmer in her eyes was promising. He doubted he was misreading her interest.

He opened the door for her. Once she climbed in, he walked over to his side. His hands were hot as anticipation burned through him, a desperate yearning to touch her again.

Touch more of her.

Once they were in his truck, the mood shifted with a single, hungry glance. The desire in her eyes mirrored his need. They lunged for each other almost at once, as if they'd been holding back for far too long.

He grabbed her face and kissed her, not caring they were in a parking lot where anyone could see them. Within minutes, they were spread across the front seat. He ran his hands down the side of her body and she reached beneath his shirt.

She pulled away, breathless. "Can we go to your place? I have roommates."

Shit. "I'm in the house with my mom and sister right now."

"Hmm," she said. "Let me see if my place is free."

She pulled out her phone and began texting while his mind

raced, considering where they could go. Not his truck. They weren't teenagers. He gritted his teeth. A hotel? Damn, he had to get his own place and soon.

Vivi exhaled with a relieved whoosh. "No one's at my apartment. Let's go there."

He could barely focus on anything else besides the promise of what might lie ahead. On the drive to her place, she appeared to be just as eager. She kissed his neck and stroked his thigh, which hardened his already semi-erect cock.

"If you keep doing that," he teased, "It's going to steer the car itself."

She chuckled. Damn, he loved to hear her laugh, especially when he was the one to make her do so.

After circling the area a few times, he found a spot. Once he parked, they stumbled to her front door, kissing and pawing at each other on the way.

Someone shouted, "Get a room!"

She laughed against his throat, before murmuring, "We're working on it."

Inside, he noticed mismatched furniture in the living room, a couch and two arm chairs. The usual student variety, perhaps second-hand from a family member or picked up a thrift store. She led him through the door into her bedroom.

Vivi's room.

"Here we are," she said. "My humble abode. Better than the barracks or a camp, but not the Ritz."

He paused a moment to take it in. This was where Vivi lived, slept every night. The faint scent of cinnamon hung in the air, which he attributed to a glassed candle on her end table. Her bed was made with a white comforter and pale blue accent pillows, and her dresser was tidy. No clothes were strewn about —an effect of years in the military with routine inspections. He wasn't here to assess her tidiness, though. All he wanted was to get closer to her.

"Very ritzy," he agreed with a nod.

She giggled. "Want a drink?" she asked. "I have white wine in the fridge."

"No." He stepped up to her and cupped her face with both hands. "All I want is right here."

Her eyes flickered with excitement and dark lust. "I've wanted this for so long, Jack. Don't make me wait any longer."

He didn't need any more of an invitation to spur back into action. When he kissed her, he all but plundered her mouth.

She responded in kind, matching his rhythm in a desperate chase to get closer. He explored as much of her as he could reach. She ran her hands down his body. When her fingers stroked his erection, it was a wonder he didn't explode into his pants. He pressed himself against her, itching to break through the clothes separating them.

Leading her back toward the bed, they fell together, landing in a clumsy heap on top of her comforter. So much for a smooth seduction.

She laughed and pushed her hair away from her face. "That was on me. My balance isn't what it used to be."

The last thing he was going to do was draw attention to the reason. He slid over her and kissed her neck, and then reached under her dress, which was fortunately made of some stretchy fabric. He stroked her belly. "That was what I'd call a perfectly choreographed move," he murmured. "We ended up right where I wanted to be."

He pulled up the dress and trailed kisses above the seam of her leggings, around her belly button. Her breath caught and then she sighed.

Reaching up, he squeezed her breast. She squirmed under his mouth and arched her body.

Time to remove the obstacles. He wanted them to be skin to skin, needed to touch all of her—and taste. Fuck, he'd wanted to taste her for so long. If he didn't tonight, he'd lose a battle holding on to his sanity. She was too close, too tempting.

He pulled her dress up over her head. "I can't wait to see you, Vivi. All of you." When he started to pull her tights down, she tensed.

She placed her hand on his. "Wait."

"What's wrong?" he asked.

She bit her lip and her expression turned worried. "I'm afraid."

CHAPTER 8

VIVI

Vivi had existed in a delirious state as Jack trailed kisses over her body. The familiar comfort of her bedroom set the scene for what she had fantasized about for so long.

Raw need had mixed with pleasure. But when he'd moved down to her tights, a vivid reminder of what she'd expose to him returned. He's caught a glimpse of her scars the night of the gala, but he'd be seeing her—*all* of her. Those ugly, vicious gashes that marked her as damaged.

"What are you afraid of, Vivi?" Jack's voice was gentle.

"Showing you my scars." She swallowed. "They're not pretty."

"Don't be." He kissed her palm. "They're just scars. We all have them. Some on the inside, some out. They don't make you any less beautiful."

After she gave him a skeptical look, he continued. "They show you're more than just the beauty on the surface. You're brave. Amazing. You earned those scars during a mission many people would be too chicken shit to volunteer for."

She took a long, slow breath. That was one of the kindest things she'd heard in a while. She sighed. "That means a lot to me."

"You're worried that I'll judge you because of them. I can see it on your face." He kissed her wrist. "But I'm in awe of how someone as amazing as you are, Vivi, would let me into her life."

A swell of emotions rose in her. Nobody had put it to her that way before.

Jack caressed her arm and down her side, planting soft kisses on the way. He took his time with slow movements, waiting for her to grow more comfortable. Soon she was hot again with need, eager to continue.

When he moved his mouth down to her hips, she squirmed. "I think I'd be more comfortable with the lights down."

He searched her nightstand. She had a few Yankee Candle jars around the room. "How about candlelight?"

That might work. The low light of the flame could be flattering.

Or it could distort an already marred image.

Stop freaking out. You want this. Don't let your hang-ups kill it because you know damn well you'll regret it, just like you regretted not going for it in the past.

"Yes, let's light some candles," she agreed.

He reached for the lighter on the end table and lit the closest one, apple and cinnamon, followed by the smaller pumpkin ones beside it. After climbing out of bed, he lit another one on her bureau, followed by the others until. The fragrances of autumn in New England soon infused the room like a soothing caress.

Jack's consideration touched her. He didn't dismiss her insecurities as ridiculous. She needed time to adjust and he gave her all he needed.

She was one lucky woman.

He turned out the light and sat beside her. Soft candlelight blanketed the space near the bed, highlighting his chiseled face.

Cupping her face in his hands, he said, "You are beautiful, Vivi. Inside and out. You always have been."

Her already rapid pulse sputtered. Hell, it had gone out of control since the moment Jack strode back into her life.

When he pressed his lips to hers, she practically liquefied. She moved closer to him, wanting more, but he pulled back.

"I know you're afraid." He searched her eyes. "I am, too."

She furrowed her brows. What could strong and steady Jack possibly be afraid of? "Of what?"

He took two low breaths before answering. "I'm scared of how strong my feelings are for you." His voice lowered so she barely heard him. "It's all happened so fast between us, and I'm so confused about many things in my life right now, but I know in here that this is right." The volume in his tone grew with certainty. He placed one strong hand on his broad chest. "Maybe it's because we've known each other in the past that we skipped all that early getting-to-know-you jazz. You know me —you get me in all the important ways. You even know my fear. Except one."

His eyes appeared so vulnerable, somehow more so by candlelight. Vivi wanted to reach out and do something to comfort him.

She stroked his arm. "What's that?"

"That this is just a flash of how happy we could be. I don't want to blow it. And if you think some scars are going to send me running, think again." He shook his head and then caressed her cheek. "They only make me admire you more."

Her heart, long-suffering from all the cardio these past few days, seized up as she listened intently to each word. *Breathe. Respond.*

What could she say to that? There were no words. She fought to find something, anything.

"You know all the right things to say, Jack," she sighed. "I wish I could do the same for you."

"You don't have to say anything."

But she could show him how much he meant to her. She touched his cheek, loving the feel of his stubble on her hand. Searching his eyes before she leaned forward and her lids closed. She kissed him again, this time not holding anything back.

When they broke apart to breathe, she pulled up her dress over her head. He watched her with an intense expression. As she removed her bra, his eyes smoldered. No one had ever looked at her with such raw hunger and yearning, and it stoked a new wave of desire flooding through her.

Jack leaned her back onto the bed and claimed her mouth with a deep kiss. He moved his hands over her throat, shoulders, and then breasts. She moaned her pleasure.

He lowered his mouth to kiss and suck each one, and her skin tingled with need. God, she'd wanted this for so long. She arched her body, never wanting him to stop.

When he moved his hands over her skin and reached her leggings, she took a fortifying breath. This was it. She removed them slowly, anticipation heightening every passing second, as she exposed herself to him.

He continued to ramp up her excitement with his hands and mouth traveling over her torso with slow, deliberate torture. When he reached her legs, she stilled, fearing the worst.

He lowered his head and kissed over the scars, the raw red and vivid white slashes that would forever mark her. "You're exquisite."

The worst was over. She exhaled and released the remaining tension that had held her muscles hostage.

The uncertainty of his response was no longer a factor. He

hadn't recoil with revulsion. She allowed herself to let go and enjoy the experience she'd yearned for.

He continued to explore up her legs, focusing on her inner thighs until she was squirming and panting under his featherlight kisses, her senses turning haywire.

When he finally moved between her legs, where she desperately needed him to be, a strangled sound escaped her. He licked her with a long, languid stroke that made her shudder with a heaving sigh.

His slow strokes grew more intense as he gripped her hips more tightly. She didn't care about anything except what he was doing, and how right this felt. If this was the reward for all that time of waiting, she'd gladly wait for five times that amount.

Hell no, she wouldn't. Now that she'd had a taste of how good this was, she wasn't going to let him go any time soon.

She moaned. He knew how to play her body just right. Either he was a skillful lover or an intuitive one, because he appeared to know what she wanted before she did. He alternated using the broad part of his tongue and the tip, circling her sensitive flesh or applying greater pressure on her clit. Whenever she rose, he'd pull back before pushing her higher again.

He had her on the edge, to a point where she'd go delirious if he pulled back this time. "Don't stop," she begged. "Please."

This time, he didn't tease her. He increased the pressure until she was soaring. She raised her hips and clutched at his shoulders and then the sheets, seeking to hold on to something as she slipped, lost into a whirlwind of pleasure. She cried out as she reached the peak and hovered as the tremendous force gripped her—and then she crashed over the edge.

Wave after wave of pleasure soared through her. He relaxed the pressure as they ebbed, but didn't pull away.

After a few more seconds, he revved her up again. This time, she shot up so quickly and shattered with such an explosive impact, she thought she'd never recover. He remained between her legs, unrelenting. Like he couldn't get enough of her.

"Jack, please." She reached for his shoulders. "I need you."

"Need me how?" he murmured.

"You know how." He was going to torture her, wasn't he? "Inside me."

He tore off his clothes. The sudden absence of his body almost made her whimper until she took in the sight—broad chest, carved abs, muscular thighs, and a very impressive erection.

In between rough pants, she asked, "Condom?"

"Right," he replied with a low groan.

He reached inside his pants pocket. She waited with breathless anticipation as he covered himself with one.

Jack crawled over her and repositioned himself, grinding against her.

"You're so wet," he murmured.

"I want you." This was it, the moment she'd yearned for.

Jack kissed her and she tasted herself on his tongue. He pulled back and locked his eyes on her as he slid the tip in. She moaned as he entered, clinging to his back as he stretched her. He gradually pushed in, a welcome and mind-blowing invasion.

He paused. "You okay?"

"Don't stop," she begged.

He pushed slowly, letting her adjust to his girth. And then he was in, filling her with a delicious sensation.

He paused. "Fuck, you feel so good, Vivi."

She relished the sensation of having him there, holding him tight, unwilling to let him go. When he moved, she loosened her death grip. As he filled her, the sensual pain turned into pleasure. She moved against him, increasing the friction with each deep thrust. He'd started out gentle, but then drove into her deeper and harder, and her panting escalated to low squeals.

How long had it been since she'd felt like this?

Never. Because it had never been with Jack. It felt—*right*. It was silly to think that way, but her body told her otherwise. She wanted to scream in exhilaration. This wasn't another damn fantasy, but the real thing. She'd wanted this for so long and her dreams had become reality at last, more satisfying than any fantasy.

Sex was enjoyable, most of the time, but this was on a different level. Beyond a physical response. She was brimming with happiness—delirious happiness.

How could sex bring out such jubilance?

When he shoved into her so hard that she dug her nails into him with a desperate cry, she couldn't think anymore, couldn't argue with herself. All she could do was hold on as he drove her higher, pushing her into a primal state where thoughts melted away.

Vivi raised her hips, loving the increased friction at this angle as he drove into her. The stirrings of an orgasm teased her from a distance. She grabbed him tighter, clinging to him as the pressure rose and rose.

"Let me on top," she suggested. She hadn't done that position that often, but he brought something out in her that made her want to claim her desires.

His eyes glimmered with dark excitement. "Hold on." He held on to her as he rolled them over, keeping her on top of him, yet he slipped out of her at the very end.

His sudden absence left her aching with need, but he drove himself back inside her within a heartbeat. The heat in his stare appeared more intense by candlelight. His lust fueled hers, killing any remaining inhibitions.

She glided down on him, savoring how his shaft stroked every sensitive nerve. While she circled and ground against him, he gripped her hips and plunged into her from below, hitting her just right.

Nothing else mattered but this moment that drowned out the world. Overpowering. Leaving her spellbound.

The rising climax rushed through her with such force she cried out. She dropped her head back, closed her eyes, and whimpered as the intensity splintered her.

"Yeah, come for me, baby," Jack encouraged with a low, velvety rumble.

Pleasure rocked through her, stilling the outside world. Thoughts didn't exist any longer, only physical needs and the pure pleasure of release.

Jack continued to drive into her with a wild, frantic pace. She opened her eyes and rejoined him in rhythm, sensing he was right on the edge with her.

He gripped her hips tightly as he hammered into her with greater force. His expression was fierce and determined, and it excited her on some deep, primal level. He slammed into her with a furious thrust and dropped his head back onto her pillow, letting out a low groan. His cock throbbed into her as he pumped out his release.

He wrapped his arms around her, pulling her on top of him. She nestled in the damp space near his neck, breathing in his heated masculine scent. Their hearts continued to beat against each other in a wild, frantic dance.

Vivi couldn't speak, didn't think she ever could again. One thought bubbled up amid the haze of lust. She couldn't just potentially fall in love with Jack.

She already was halfway there.

CHAPTER 9

JACK

After the night with Vivi, Jack woke eager for a repeat the next morning. How could he not want to touch her again? She slept on her side, facing him. Sunlight fell across her face and her back rose as if in deep sleep. She looked like an angel and appeared so at peace, he didn't dare disturb her.

He glanced around her room, something he hadn't paid much attention to last night when all his focus was on her. A few books on her nightstand and framed photos on the dresser were lined up evenly. A handful of frog trinkets and photos caught his eye. Interesting. He'd never met anyone who had a thing for frogs. He'd have to ask her about it.

Several minutes later, she stirred and opened her eyes, and he forgot about the frogs.

"Good morning, beautiful." He kissed her cheek.

He couldn't stop himself from touching her again. Everywhere. She was all gentle curves and soft skin. The softest of all was between her legs. Shit, she felt like hot, wet silk. And she tasted so fucking good, he wanted to feast on her once more.

So he did. Kissing and licking from her neck down. Over her breasts. Her belly. Down.

As he lowered his head between her legs, she relaxed onto her bed. "Oh, what a way to wake up," she murmured.

Indeed. He'd be happy to start the day with Vivi like this every morning. Although she'd been tense at first last night, this morning, she was relaxed and let him know exactly what she liked. Soon she was moaning and clutching at the sheets. When he brought her to a climax, she cried out his name.

After she recovered, she said. "Jack, you're killing me. If a woman can die from a multitude of orgasms in one night, that is."

He loved being the one to bring her to that state. "It's a new day so we start over. And I'm so hard, I don't want to climb out of this bed without being with you once more."

Her eyelids lowered as she gave him a suggestive glance. "I'm yours all morning."

Jack didn't need to hear that invitation twice. After sheathing himself with a condom, he lowered his body onto hers, sliding against her warm, wet flesh. He nestled against her neck, inhaling the scent of her damp skin, and then slid inside her welcoming channel. She felt incredible, and he knew he wouldn't last long this morning. But he wanted to make her come once more.

He drove into her, pinning her against the bed, and she wrapped her arms and legs around him. He lifted her off the mattress and this new angle made her wild. She gripped onto him with a tighter hold as she rose higher and higher and then climaxed with a gasp on her lips.

He soon followed, emptying himself into her with a guttural moan.

They lay panting, damp limbs draped over each other, as

their heart rates slowed. He trailed his fingers over her soft skin, savoring the moment. Being with her felt *right*.

Since he'd returned home, something had seemed off, but that feeling vanished when he was with Vivi. He didn't feel so unsteady, so lost.

She'd told him he had her all morning, but that wasn't long enough. He didn't want to let her go anytime soon. Maybe he could convince her to cancel her plans.

Bad idea. He wasn't doing it again, trying to control the situation. Time to redirect on to something else.

His gaze fell on one of her frog trinkets.

"What's with all the frogs?"

"I bought a few in my travels. Not sure why…something about them I liked. It became a running thing with my family getting me a frog every Christmas and birthday. It's out of control now. I have a shoebox full of them in my closet."

The personal connection with her family made him look at her in a new light. There was much to be discovered. "Shows they care about you, right?"

"True."

A closing door outside her room made him jerk his head.

"Just my roommate leaving for work," Vivi said. "Hungry?"

He could eat. "Ravenous. Sustenance, woman. I need sustenance," he teased. "You've taken all my energy."

"Likewise." She smiled.

When they went into the small, bright kitchen with white cabinets and a round table, she nodded at him. "There are eggs in the fridge. Can you make yourself useful while I scrounge up some other food?"

He grinned and nodded. "Scrambled eggs, coming up."

They pulled together breakfast with eggs, toast, cantaloupe, and some coffee. As they ate, they talked about their day ahead. She had coursework and had to walk a couple of dogs. She had a few gigs taking care of other people's pets while they were at work.

"Can I see you again tonight?" he asked.

She arched a brow. "After last night and this morning, I think you can convince me to do just about anything."

* * *

Jack spent much of the next week at Vivi's place. While she had classes and her pet gigs during the day, he kept himself busy. He browsed online for job and housing options. Since he'd saved up money for a down payment, he looked at both real estate sales and rentals, but it didn't make sense to buy if he wasn't staying in Boston for long. In the evenings, they got together, eating out or in, depending on her roommate situation.

One night, they ate at a café on the Boston Harbor with a view of the twinkling waters. They then walked off their meal walking along the waterfront, stopping by to visit the harbor seals at the outdoor tank at the New England Aquarium. They then meandered over to Faneuil Hall and Quincy Market and stopped for a drink at one of the pubs.

Another night, they went a movie house for an X-Files marathon. After they left the theater and wandered through the streets of Cambridge, he turned to her.

He glanced at their surroundings near MIT in the bustle of Kendall Square and then lowered his voice just above a whisper. "I never told this to anyone before—but when I was seven, I saw a strange light outside my bedroom window. When I looked out to observe what it was, I saw this egg-shaped orb in the distance. It looked like it was hovering, flames at the base—"

Vivi waved her arms and shook her head. "Nope, nope, nope. Don't even start."

"Start what?" he declared with mock innocence.

"You're going to spin some tale about a UFO." She wagged her finger. "I know you, Jack Conroy. I haven't forgotten about the Sasquatch story. I'm not falling for this."

He laughed, caught before he could even finish his tale, and pulled her close to him. "Yes, you do." Then he kissed her.

THE NEXT DAY, HE TRIED A GYM THAT WASN'T FAR FROM VIVI'S. He wasn't ready to join any with long-term commitments, since he didn't know where he'd end up living, but staying in shape was one of his priorities. Just as he'd finished an upper-body workout and had showered off, he had a call from an old buddy in the Marines.

After they caught up briefly, Stevens said, "I heard you might be looking for a job."

"Yeah, I'm back in Boston, exploring my options," Jack replied.

"I might have something you'd be interested in."

After days of lackluster findings in the job listings, Jack was keen to hear more. "What's that?"

"I need a project manager down here in DC," Stevens said. "We want someone with military experience and leadership skills for some training initiatives we're putting together. You'd be perfect for the job. But you'd need to relocate."

Damn, that offer was unexpected. They spent the next several minutes going over the details. It had an educational component that appealed to him and with his recent military experience, it was a perfect fit. On paper, at least.

DC was an exciting city. It would be a great place to start the next phase in his career.

A twinge at the back of his neck made him rub at the tension. What was with the discomfort?

He took a deep breath and exhaled. It would mean moving again. Away from his family. Away from home.

Away from Vivi.

"Think about it," Stevens said. "Can you get back to me by the end of next week?"

"Will do. Thanks for thinking of me, man."

All afternoon, he debated the pros and cons of the move. Career-wise, it was a great offer. He could picture himself excelling in that role. But…

His shoulders sagged. A big con was leaving Boston and three women he cared about. One he'd only reconnected with less than two weeks ago.

Was that long enough to have an impact on a major life decision? Probably not.

That evening, Jack brought Chinese takeout to Vivi's apartment. After he greeted her with a deep kiss, she poured them each a glass of Chardonnay and they took their usual chairs at the small kitchen table.

A bright yellow headband pushed her shiny brown hair behind her shoulders and down her back. It was a shade brighter than the soft yellow sweater that looked like cashmere. So pretty. With the jeans and black boots, she looked like a typical college student. Although with her military background, there was nothing average about her.

They sat across the small kitchen table tucked against the wall and ate. As they caught up about their days, he told her about the call. While he spoke, she'd stopped eating her lo mein.

"What do you think?" he asked her.

She took a sip of wine. Once she placed the glass down, she shifted in the kitchen chair. "Do you want to take the job?"

He tried to read into her reaction. Her tone didn't reveal much. She'd kept it neutral. She attempted to do so with her expression, but he detected a flash of disappointment.

Would she want him to stay?

"I'm not sure. A part of me does. It would be a good opportunity." He stabbed some noodles, spinning them around his fork. "The other part doesn't."

Vivi leaned forward. "Why not?"

He chewed and swallowed before replying. "I've been gone for years, and now I'm home." He dropped his fork. The indecision killed his appetite. "I thought I'd settle down here. Not run off again, like this is just another leave."

She gave him a gentle look. "I can understand that."

"Plus," he added. "There's you."

"Oh." She covered her heart and shook her head. "Jack, you can't give up a great opportunity because of me. We've only just started dating."

He knew that, but she'd already become a big part of his life. "I understand that. What do you think I should do?"

Vivi averted his gaze, gazing beyond him. She shook her head. "I can't answer that question. Only you know what's right for you."

IN HER BED THAT NIGHT, JACK SENSED A DIFFERENT TONE between them. The playful, magical time together of getting to know each other better and exploring each other's bodies had shifted, reminding him of how moments in the Marines could turn from lighthearted to serious in a flash. That discussion had made him consider the significance of their relationship. Did it for Vivi as well?

If he took the job in DC, their relationship would change, maybe even end. They could try to make a long-distance relationship work—if she'd even go for that.

He took his time caressing her body, worshipping every soft angle and curve. Their time together could be cut short, and if so, he wanted to remember every moment of it.

After they both climaxed, he spooned her. She fell asleep in his arms, the soft sounds of her deep breaths and alluring scent soothing him. Still, he couldn't fall into a restful sleep with all the questions burning in his mind.

One centered on her. Did she still do the things she loved, like rock climbing? He wanted to ask her about it, yet be careful not to set upset her.

The next morning, he resolved to get out of his head for a while. She had plenty of obstacles to deal with since coming home, much more than his silly problems. How did she manage to face them?

While they prepared a quick breakfast with bagels and coffee, he rehearsed variations in his head. Dancing around the topic would only make her suspicious, so he went for a direct question.

He poured her coffee in a mug with three kittens in the See No Evil, Hear No Evil, Speak No Evil poses and handed it to her. "Have you gone rock climbing since you've been back?"

Vivi had been spreading cream cheese on her bagel. She froze for a couple of seconds before resuming at a quicker speed. "No."

Jack suspected that, as well as her not being eager to discuss it. "Why not?"

Her expression hardened. Shit, he had to be careful. He was moving onto unsteady ground.

"You know why." She put the knife down and turned to him, ponytail spinning. "My leg."

He kept his tone gentle. "That shouldn't stop you. You danced with me."

She arched her brows and then snorted. "Clumsily." She carried her bagel from the counter to the table and sat. "And that was with two feet on the ground."

Jack carried his mug and bagel over and sat across from her. He didn't want her to dismiss it without giving it a try. "If it would help, they have adaptive gear. I've heard about programs focused on getting vets climbing."

"I *don't* want to do that."

With her resolute tone, he was definitely moving into minefield territory. One false step might blow up his entire plan. "You loved it, Vivi. Why give up something you loved when you can find a way to do it again?"

Her gaze drifted off into the distance, as if lost in her own thoughts.

She pursed her lips before replying, "It won't be the same."

He could practically read the subtext—*she wasn't the same*. Was anyone after they faced such an ordeal?

"You're a Marine, Vivi. You always will be," he encouraged with a squeeze of her hand. "And Marines adapt and overcome, no matter what the challenge."

She snatched her hand back and gritted her teeth. She raised her gaze to meet them, anger flashing in her eyes. "Don't give me that line. I've heard all the ooh-rah crap—*Ready to die but never will* and all that. That's bullshit. They die all the time. It's one thing to spout sayings to get them motivated to fight, but it's another to tell someone who's had the blood of a dead teammate on her. Something I think about every goddamn day."

He knew that feeling all too well. One of his lance corporals, Martin, had bled out. His blood had spilled through Jack's fingers before the corpsman took over. The truth grew agonizingly clear as the puddle of red in the sand grew larger...

Now wasn't the time to think about it, so he shoved back in its proper compartment. He gritted his teeth and focused on what she'd said. He pushed her way over the fuckin' line. At least she was talking about what had happened, rather than bottling it up the way he did.

"I'm sorry, Vivi. You're right."

She didn't say anything for a long moment. "I don't want to

have to wear anything that announces that I'm different. The limp is bad enough."

"It's not that noticeable. It took me awhile to even see it."

"*I* know it's there. And I hate not being able to do what I once could."

Her voice softened to a lower tone and the vulnerability in it tugged at him.

"I get that. But you can find another way to enjoy it without comparing it to what you could do before." He raised both hands, palms facing her. "Hear me out for a minute, okay?"

She crossed her arms and leaned back in the chair. "Okay."

"There's a new facility not far from here. Let's just go and check it out," Jack suggested with a casual wave as if it were no big deal. "You could try a beginner bouldering wall to get a feel for it."

She stared down into her mug.

"I'll be there with you, Vivi," he swore. "I won't let anything happen."

She blew out a breath. "I'll think about it."

"Don't worry," he added. "I'll be right there watching your back."

"*If* I go."

"You'll go."

"What makes you so sure?" She fixed a questioning stare on him, one edged with worry.

He gave her a satisfied smile. "Because I know you. You're tough, determined, and stubborn. A setback isn't enough to hold you down. Besides, I'll be there. Ready to catch you if you need me."

The anxiety in her expression vanished as her face broke into a one-sided grin. "You're a cocky son of a bitch, aren't you, Conroy?"

"Some people might say so." He winked.

"*I* might be one of them."

"It's just a visit."

"Ugh, you're not going to leave me alone about this, will you?"

"Tell you what, you try it tonight, and I'll clean out every litter box during your next shift at the shelter."

Her expression turned triumphant as she extended a hand. "That happens to be tomorrow morning. You've got yourself a deal."

He shook her hand, satisfied with his progress. "I'll pick you up back here later on. Is four o'clock good?"

"Yes, my last class ends at 2:30."

"Perfect."

"Wait," she said. "If I'm going to put myself out there, taking a chance, so should you."

"With what?"

She gave him a look that seemed to pierce right into his soul. "Think about it. I'm sure you'll find something."

Her reply raised more questions than answers. What did she see that he was missing?

CHAPTER 10

VIVI

*I*n her last class of the day, a history lecture, Vivi twirled her pen and questioned why she'd agreed to try rock climbing. She suspected it had everything to do with Jack Conroy. Damn, he was pushy. And confident—one of the things about him that was so alluring.

Perhaps he was right. She needed to get out of her slump and try things once again. She'd settled into her routine, so the idea of trying something new had an exciting appeal.

Especially with him as part of the deal.

But for how long? With this job offer, he might be out of her life just as soon as he'd stepped into it. She put her pen down, but then shifted into tapping her foot.

It was foolish for her to grow as close to him as she'd been. Even more ridiculous to think they might have been building something more.

She clearly needed to back up and get a grip on reality.

Throughout the afternoon, she became aware of her scars.

They now pulsed with a sense of heat. That often happened before a storm. But the skies outside the window of the lecture hall appeared to be a calm and peaceful blue.

She chalked it up to nerves and resumed twirling her pen.

When Jack picked her up at her apartment at four, the familiar tingles returned that often came out whenever she was near him. Like a wild but pleasant fluttering in her stomach.

He glanced down at her outfit. "You look fantastic."

She'd put on athletic leggings, a tank top, and jacket. Nothing alluring. Still, hot shivers ran along her skin. He could melt icicles with that dark, velvety tone.

"Thanks." It was time for her to fortify herself mentally for the challenge ahead. "Let's do this."

Twenty minutes later, she stepped into the rock climbing gym. The familiar scent of chalk greeted her and speakers blasted an upbeat song.

But then everything changed. All the excitement from earlier dissipated as if someone had pierced a balloon with a hatchet.

Her stomach hardened and churned. Climbers at various heights and difficulty levels reached for colorful holds positioned around the walls, belayed by their partners. *She'd* be Jack's partner. She didn't know if she could climb, let alone support him. Doubts rose within as quickly as all those fit climbers pushing their way up the walls.

Could she do it?

No.

To punctuate her misgivings, her scars pulsed with a faint throbbing.

While Jack stepped up to the front desk, she froze in place. He turned and walked back to her. She probably stood like an out-of-place statue.

"I can't do this," she admitted.

"Why not?" His expression was etched with concern for her. When she didn't respond, he added in a lower volume, "Is your leg bothering you?"

"It's not that." She stared at a woman climbing one of the tougher climbs—something Vivi used to be able to do. Not any longer. Her heart hammered, and her skin turned clammy.

"We can get you adaptive gear and a trainer to help, Viv, if you need it," Jack suggested.

"No." She shook her head vigorously. "It's more than the proper equipment."

He prodded, "Tell me."

She ran her hands over the loose strands of hair that had slipped out of her ponytail. "This was a bad idea. I can't do this."

"Of course you can," Jack encouraged. "Using different equipment doesn't change anything. We all have our weaknesses and need support."

He didn't get it. He couldn't. "That's easy for you to say. You don't know what it's like, Jack. You're whole. Beautiful. Not damaged like me."

He stared at her for several long heartbeats that seemed to echo in her ear and then gave her hand a gentle squeeze. "Nobody comes home unaffected. If they say they are, they're either full of shit or lying to themselves."

His intense expression almost made her forget why she had reservations.

"But you're right, Vivi," he continued. "I don't know what it's like for you. What I do know is that you're a natural, a bad ass, and you loved to climb in Okinawa. I'd hate to see you give up something you love when you could do it again with some modifications."

His voice sounded muffled as she scanned the walls again and the colors blended into streaks. The last time they climbed together, she'd been fearless, eager to tackle the most advanced routes. Her scars throbbed now. There was no way she'd be able to do it. She would fail. Even worse, she'd *fail* in front of *Jack*—glaring proof she wasn't a good match for him.

"I know other vets who have been injured," he continued. "My cousin, Matty, was a SEAL, and is now back in Newport after he suffered leg injuries as well. It took time but he's able to run again. He even worked up to running the stairs all the way around Harvard Stadium, which he loves to do when he comes up to visit." Jack paused and added, "I admire him. I admire anyone who takes on challenges that are easy for the rest of us, ones we take for granted. That's what I think of as bravery."

Maybe Jack was trying to inspire her by talking about others, but she couldn't hear it. It just undermined what a coward she was at the moment.

"Clearly, I'm not one of them since I'm not acting brave right now." She backed up, breath coming in quicker as she moved toward the exit. "I don't want the world to see how messed up I am.

"I'm self-conscious," she added. "Maybe it's stupid and superficial, but I hate it when people stare at me with pity. I can practically see the gears in their brains moving as they wonder what happened." She pointed at him. "I even saw it with you the night of the gala when you saw my scars."

Vivi reached the front door while Jack simply gaped at her with a confused expression.

She turned and shoved the door open. Once outside, she gulped the crisp autumn air.

"Vivi—"

Jack must have followed her outside.

"No, please." She put her arm behind her, refusing to look back.

"But—"

She sensed she was overreacting, that she was on the verge of a panic attack, but couldn't stop the terror that rushed through her like a sniper's bullet. It pinpointed to one narrow instinct—get out of this situation.

"It's nobody's goddamn business what happened to me," she snapped. "You should forget you ever ran into me. I can only hold you back."

"Vivi, wait. Let's talk about this."

"What for? It doesn't change anything, Jack." She threw her hands in the air and dropped them at her sides. "You should move on. Consider that job in DC."

Did she really say all that? Was she freaking out on such an epic level that she'd *end* their relationship over this?

Yes. She'd been deluding herself since the ball. Who did she think she was—Cinderella being swept away by her prince? Ha, fat chance. She was a wounded vet who didn't believe in fairy tales. Life wasn't like that.

In the end, it came down to compatibility, and that's where she and Jack fell apart. He had the world ahead of him—he already had this great job opportunity in DC. But her injury had hampered not only her abilities, but opportunities for her future.

"Don't go," Jack pleaded.

She had to. It was for the best. For both of them.

"This whole thing was a mistake." She took two deep breaths and forced herself to meet his eyes. It's over, Jack. Please—," she stammered. "Please leave me alone."

She turned away from him and rushed down the sidewalk, her limp taunting her by slowing down her desperate urge to escape.

The intrusive image flashed in her brain. The sudden explosion. The bright light. The boom.

She squeezed her eyes shut for a second as if she could force it to recede.

Her breath came hard. Her skin turned cold with sweat. She took deep breaths to counter the impending attack.

Just breathe. It will pass. Just breathe. It will pass.
She repeated the mantra to cling to control.

Her heart thrashed like it was about to claw out of her chest.

She progressed to the next coping method and pictured her happy place. Inside the cat shelter, there was no war, no explosives, no one trying to kill them—just cats seeking food and sometimes affection. She visualized stroking their soft fur and how their purrs vibrated beneath her fingers.

The image helped calm her chaotic systems. She held on to it as she made her way home, holding onto something as the world around her crumbled.

JACK

Jack stared at Vivi as she walked away from him. Her limp was more pronounced now that she was upset and rushing, which tugged at him all the more.

She appeared so alone in that moment, a silhouette disappearing into the shadows. Another lost soul in the city.

Just like him.

Was she walking out of his life for good?

That's what exactly what she'd said.

He followed her for a few steps, searching for the words that would make it right. None came, so he halted. Chasing her wouldn't do any good, especially since she so clearly wanted to get away from him. He'd practically tripped over a tripwire and had his plans blow up in his face.

Wow, that was smooth. You pushed her, and she left. Even worse, she ended it. You couldn't see that one coming?

When she turned around the corner of the brick exterior of the gym, it took all his willpower to keep his feet planted. She didn't want him to follow her, that much was clear. She didn't even want to talk to him. He tightened his hands into fists and took some deep breaths to get a hold of the situation.

The air felt weighted with moisture, but not as heavy as the regret settling in his gut.

His sister's words replayed in his head, how he pushed people to do what he thought was best for them. Maybe she was right. Although he meant well, his vision was too narrow-minded. What he thought was best wasn't necessarily what they wanted. And boom—sometimes his best intentions imploded.

Is that what he'd done here?

He grunted. The answer was clearly yes, considering Vivi's reaction.

Would she be all right getting home? He'd driven her so he should be driving her back. But she'd told him to leave her alone. For good.

Fuck.

As he walked to the truck, he wrestled with what to do next. The residential neighborhood appeared quiet and relatively safe, but that didn't mean shit. Something could happen anytime, anywhere.

And if anything happened to Vivi, it would kill him.

Climbing into his truck, he stared down the street. What the hell should he do now?

Fuck it. He put the truck in drive and followed her. He had to make sure she got home safely.

His truck was black, hardly distinguishable from the half dozen others on the same road. It wasn't like it was a glaring orange VW bug that would stand out. Once he turned the corner, he spotted her. He parked in a free space. When she walked out of sight, he drove on and repeated the action at another parking spot.

Like a damn stalker.

But he wasn't stalking her, he was making sure she got home safely. It was his responsibility since he brought her here, right?

Never once did she turn back. No sign of regret, of wanting

to return to him. The finality in her determination kicked him hard in the gut.

Memories of their nights together returned. The softness of her skin. How she tasted. The sounds she made when he was deep inside her. How good it felt.

How *right* they were together.

Watching her walk away from him was torture, an echo of her final declaration for him to leave her alone. He'd never be with her again, never have that bliss they'd found in each other's arms.

He should have known better. They were doomed. Had been from the start. It was one obstacle after another with them. How many signs did one person need before they took the fuckin' hint?

A few rain drops landed on his windshield. Gray clouds now loomed overhead, piercing through the blue sky. Brilliant, now it was about to rain.

He had to pull up to her and offer her a ride. He couldn't let her walk in it. Ah, but then she'd know he followed her, and that would piss her off even more.

He could hear her in his head reaming him out, telling him she was not a delicate freakin' flower and a few damn raindrops wouldn't stop her.

What if he drove up and said something corny about the rain to lighten the mood?

Ha, with the way she hurried ahead, arms swinging at her sides and limping more than he'd ever seen, she didn't appear to be in a receptive mood for his bad jokes. Now was clearly not the time. She was hurting and needed space.

Still, he followed her home, resisting the agony of not being able to do something. No point trying to save someone who didn't want to be rescued.

After he made sure she'd made it safely to the front door of her apartment and headed inside, he lingered on her street for a few more minutes. Once he drove away, it might be the last time he'd see her. They'd be over. The idea suffocated him with dread.

A part of him hoped she'd text him, saying she'd overreacted. They'd laugh about it, have a drink, and tumble into her bed. He'd spent time making her feel good to make up for his bad judgment earlier.

The minutes ticked by. While he waited, he listened to his iPhone. *Black Sabbath* came on, perfect for his dismal state.

After the full seven minutes went by, he gritted his teeth and put his truck into drive. She wanted nothing to do with him.

Still, he couldn't give up yet. Not after how right the world seemed now with her in it. Did he not make it better for her? He pictured the stark terror on her face inside the gym. Clearly not.

Maybe tomorrow, she'd wake up and feel different. If not, he'd have to find another way to reach her and make up for being such an unintentional asshole. But how?

He shook his head and said, "No fucking clue."

CHAPTER 11

VIVI

An autumn breeze swept through campus the next morning, swirling the red and brown fallen leaves. Vivi zipped her gray fleece up to her neck. The leaves crunched beneath her black boots as she walked the path to her classroom. The sunlight shone bright overhead as if mocking her bleak mood.

Why had she agreed to go with Jack to the rock climbing gym yesterday? That had been a bad idea. Caught up in the haze of lust after those nights with Jack, she'd been on a high, foolishly thinking she could take on more than she could handle.

But she couldn't. She'd had to fight off a damn panic attack fueled by that realization.

Jack would see what a mess she was, tormented by her past. Why would anyone want to deal with someone with her issues? The insomnia, the nightmares, the flashbacks.

Funny how they'd subsided since Jack came back into her

life, something she hadn't thought about until now. He had been a beautiful distraction, spoiling her with his captivating smile, odd sense of humor, and mind-blowing orgasms.

She groaned. Nothing was funny about this situation.

Vivi entered the classroom and took a seat at the back of the class. As the professor started a dry lecture, she couldn't help but compare it to the class she'd taken with Jack. His enthusiasm had rubbed off on her.

She sighed. Their relationship had crashed almost as soon as it had started.

They'd rushed in too fast. The attraction had been hard and heavy, and with the chains of their past removed, she'd gone for him like a cat in heat.

She stifled a groan. Her cat references were as bad as his jokes. She rubbed her temples. Why?

Maybe if they'd moved slower and taken their time, things might have evolved differently, and she wouldn't have freaked out like that.

Or maybe it was the surprise of the job offer—and her defense mechanisms kicking in. Was she pushing him away because it would be easier when he left?

She doodled in her notebook. Swirls and then stars. And hearts. Broken hearts.

What was she, a teenager? She had to get over this. They were better off apart.

He could follow any opportunity he wanted, without having someone like and her baggage weighing him down. She nodded to herself, justifying her actions. He loved rock climbing. That was what had brought them together, and that was something she could no longer do. He needed to find someone he could enjoy the things he loved with. She'd go back to her new normal—school, work, and the shelter.

Cats were easier to deal with than people. Sure they acted in peculiar ways, but at least they were straightforward about it in their own strange way. If they didn't want something, they let you know. They didn't push you to do something. She gave a bitter laugh—because they didn't give a shit. It didn't matter why, cats were cats, and she was happy staying in their world.

Back in her apartment that evening, Vivi curled up on her bed with a comforting cup of hot cocoa spiked with peppermint schnapps. She picked up a Robert B. Parker mystery, as she loved reading them and recognizing the references to Boston in her new city. Whenever she'd moved around in the Marines, she'd read books set in her new locations. It gave her a connection to a foreign place. Although she tried to follow the storyline, she had trouble focusing as her thoughts wandered to Jack.

As if reading her mind, he called fifteen minutes later. She stared at his name, and her pulse quickened. She forced herself to let it go to voice mail.

Self-preservation was key. She couldn't expose herself to any more pain. Why make it more difficult?

He didn't leave a message.

He'd mentioned his cousin, the SEAL, who was now able to run football stadiums. Could she develop the physical abilities to try the things she once enjoyed again, like rock climbing?

Maybe not with her leg. Every injury was different, affecting people in distinct ways. Her limp was likely a lifelong companion. And more so were the mental blocks.

Jack called again the following day. She fought the urge to answer it. How she wanted to hear his voice. The ache inside her spread, leaving a hollow feeling.

Again, he didn't leave a message.

On the third day, he called again. She gave up the battle and took the call.

"Vivi, I'm sorry. I was out of line."

She softened on hearing his voice. He'd only been trying to do something good for her, but she wasn't the right one for him.

Be strong. Don't think of now, think of the future. He'll end up disappointed one day when he understands that you're not like how you once were.

"Face it, Jack. It won't work. Please don't make it any harder than it is."

That part was true. Her apartment now reminded her of the time they'd spent together. It was ridiculous since it was so short, but it been magical. They'd been happy. Now she missed having him around—especially when alone in her bed. Memories of the time they'd shared were torture, reminders of what they'd never have again.

"Are you sure that's what you want?" His voice was gentle.

She sensed a hint of hope in his tone. A part of her wanted to scream *of course it's not*. But it was for the best.

"I'm a mess. You have all your shit together. You always have. We just don't work."

"That's not true." His voice sounded surprised by her words.

"You should find someone who can keep up with you and do the things you like to do, whether it's here or in DC." She struggled to keep her voice steady. Her breath came quick and hard. "Not someone who's going to hold you back."

"Vivi, it's not like that—"

"I need to go."

When she ended the call, her hands were shaking. She exhaled at having gotten those difficult words out.

She slumped onto her sofa and stared at the ceiling. As she replayed the conversation in her head, uncertainty followed.

Had she made a colossal mistake?

JACK

Vivi thought she was a mess? Then what was Jack? He'd been wandering around the city like a damn ghost that didn't know how to move on to the next plane of existence.

Despite his efforts to try to move on, Jack couldn't get her out of his mind. When he sought distraction by watching the History Channel or Discovery Channel, he thought of her. Whether he went on his five-mile runs or bike rides along the Charles River, he glanced at the sun twinkling on the water's surface and wondered how she was. When he wandered through Boston Common and the surrounding streets, he pictured her face and wondered where she was. What was she doing?

Did she think of him?

Before he left his house one morning, he stared at a family photo hanging in the living room while one of his mother's cats watched from her perch in front of a window. It was one of the last ones they had with his father, one of the final photos of the four of them as a family before it was torn apart by a bullet.

He'd stared at that photo every day since he'd been home as if he'd find some symbolism to enlighten him about his murky future. He'd been twelve in the photo, in that awkward state of being a preteen, both looking up to his father and starting to rebel against him, resenting when he'd deployed.

His father had the same high-and-tight Marine haircut Jack had grown accustomed to while he was in the military. He ran his hair over the rough growth now on his chin. His father and sister had dark-blue eyes while Jack shared his mother's blue-green ones. He glanced into his father's eyes, seeking insight.

Once again, none came.

Jack left the house and rode his bike along the river, consumed with thoughts about his life. He navigated through the city and into Copley Square where he locked his bike outside the impressive arched exterior of the Boston Public Library, one of his favorite spots in the city.

He entered the lobby and stared up at the mosaic tile in the arched ceilings. As he ascended the grand staircase, he paused to admire the marble lion statues. He continued his exploration, gazing at the wondrous art and architecture throughout the library. After strolling through the stacks, he perused some books at a desk with a green banker's lamp in the Bates Room.

An hour later, he entered the courtyard. He found a nook near the fountain and gazed out at the marble arches surrounding him. Vivi's words pierced him. She thought he'd be better off with someone who could keep up with him. But he cared about *her*, not a gym partner.

She thought she was damaged, but he was, too. There was nothing wrong with that. Who didn't face hardship in their lives, which affected their outlook? Didn't she know he was hurting inside as well?

He groaned. How would she? He'd never told her. That's why she thought he had his shit together—he wore a cloak of smoke and mirrors, hiding what he didn't want the world to see.

Maybe he was the coward.

That was an issue. He wanted her to trust him, yet kept things from her—the deep, dark secrets that exposed him as far from the confident Marine officer he presented to the world.

On his bike ride home, he continued to reassess his life. Vivi had challenged him to take a risk. Maybe she was right. It was time to go his own way, follow his own passions. The one he was considering was full of uncertainty. Definitely not the safe route with the good job in DC.

He returned home and stared once more at his father's image on the wall. A strangled sound escaped Jack, surprising him. Ghosts that had haunted him for so long—some since his father's death, others more recent, shoved their way into his brain, forcing themselves to be seen. Connections were forged. The guilt, the shame, the regret rising, refusing to be shoved back down into the compartment he reinforced with bad jokes and an odd sense of humor until Jack finally dealt with them.

He lay on the sofa and stared up at the ceiling, losing track of time as a few tears rolled down his face. He didn't bother to wipe them away.

When he felt lighter, he rose. The only way for Jack to step forward was to break free from the yoke of his past. He couldn't change the past or bring back the dead, but he could try to make a positive impact for the future—just like Vivi believed he could. To do so, he had to forge his own way and follow his heart.

The first step was to call Stevens and inform him of his decision. It was a killer opportunity, but the price was too high. What he wanted in his future was here. He'd been gone from his family for a good chunk of a decade. Why run off again so soon after he'd returned home?

Besides, Vivi was now in Boston. Even if she didn't want to be in a relationship with him, it comforted him to know she was nearby. He'd spent all those final months in the Marines wondering where she'd ended up in the world.

After some small talk, Jack said, "Thanks for the opportunity, but I can't take the job. I'm going to stick around here and spend time with my family."

"No problem," Stevens replied. "You were my first choice, but I get it. Family comes first."

After they ended the call, Jack felt like he'd lost weight, like he'd removed a fifty pound rucksack after a forced march. He wanted to call Vivi and tell her. Maybe over dinner or a walk? Would she even want to hear from him?

No. She'd made that clear.

He exhaled with a low whoosh and glanced around the kitchen. If he couldn't do something nice for her, he could for the other women in his life.

When his mother and Carrie returned home twenty minutes later, he announced, "I'm cooking dinner tonight."

"Did someone rewire your circuits?" Carrie replied with a smirk.

"I can make a few meals," he confirmed with arched brows.

"I'm not completely hopeless in the kitchen. There are a few dishes I can handle without causing a major inferno."

DINNER TURNED OUT TO BE EDIBLE, WHICH WAS A SUCCESS. While they chatted over the shrimp scampi and the tossed kale salad he'd made, he mentioned how he was ramping up his search for a job locally.

"I've sent out my resume for some teaching positions around here." He shrugged. "Hoping it will lead to a couple of bites."

He never told them about the DC job offer. He'd put off their questions for the past several weeks with vague replies about exploring his options. Both of them leaned forward with eager expressions.

"Give me your resume," his mom said. "I know a few people."

"Mom, I know you're trying to help," he replied, "but you work in the home health care industry. I'm trying to land a teaching position. Not much crossover."

"Besides, everything's online these days," Carrie added. She faced him. "Let's set you up with a LinkedIn profile, if you don't have one already?"

He shook his head. "Not yet."

"Trust me," his mother added. "Putting some feelers out there is key. Not everything is done with computers. Sometimes, you need to talk to people face to face. Let them know you're looking. See what they know." She took another bite of the scampi. "This is good. When you finally settle down with someone, she'll be one lucky lady."

Without a relationship with Vivi on the horizon, it was something he didn't want to think about.

. . .

THREE MORE DAYS WENT BY. WHILE HE HELPED HIS MOTHER WITH house and yard projects, thoughts of Vivi lingered with no sign that they'd ever let up.

Maybe he'd given up too easily. He was an officer who'd faced countless challenges in the field and with bureaucracy, so why not fight harder for her? Time to take one last stand, and if he ended up knocked down, riddled with bullets, at least, he'd given it his all.

First, he needed to figure out where he'd gone wrong, so he could learn from his mistake—and he thought of one person in particular who might have more insight. He drove down to Newport, Rhode Island, to visit his cousin Matty. They arranged to meet for lunch at one of the pubs on the wharf.

When Jack arrived, Matty was pacing before the restaurant, characteristic for him as he could rarely sit still. His dark hair and beard were neatly trimmed.

When he spotted Jack, he grinned and greeted him with a bro hug.

After they pulled away, Matty gave Jack one more pat on the back. "Hey cuz, how does it feel to be a civilian?"

Jack grunted. "I'm getting used to it."

"Ah," Matty acknowledged. "Transition's a bitch, isn't it?"

"Sure is." Jack exhaled with a groan.

"Let's talk about it over some food."

They entered the restaurant, and the hostess seated them at a table with a view of Newport harbor.

"How's married life?" Jack asked.

"Splendid." Matty nodded and gave Jack a conspiratorial smile. "You should give it a try."

"I don't even have a job or a place of my own yet. Hardly a catch." He pictured Matty at Vince's wedding and chuckled. "I can't believe you're the same guy who strolled around at his brother's wedding declaring that he was a tiger not ready to be tamed."

Matty raised his hands palms up. "You're never going to let me live that down, eh?"

"Course not. That performance was legendary." Jack placed his hand on his chest. "And what kind of Marine would I be if I passed on the chance to give a Navy SEAL some shit?"

"True." Matty laughed. "What can I say?" He shrugged. "This tiger found his tigress. A perfect match."

"Does that mean some cubs are on the way?" Jack teased, remembering how his aunt had been pushing not only for his cousins to settle down, but give her grandkids.

Matty groaned. "Oh no, are you teaming up with Ma? I already live with numerous roommates, most of them four-legged and furry."

Their server welcomed them and took Jack's order of a chicken sandwich and a beer. While Matty ordered, Jack gazed out to the boats bobbing side-by-side in the harbor.

After their server walked away, Jack returned his gaze to Matty. "I want to ask you something."

"Uh oh, I sense the sudden serious tone." Matty leaned back in his high-back chair. "What is it?"

Jack summarized the quick version of how he met Vivi leading to how their short-lived affair fell apart. "I thought I was encouraging her to try something she'd loved, but it backfired. I screwed up. Where did I go wrong?"

Matty made a sound of acknowledgment. "Ah, there are a lot of emotions at play, Jack. I'm not a shrink—*and I don't play one on TV*," he added in with his characteristic playful tone. "But I did pay attention to a few things during my recovery." He sounded more serious and drummed his fingers on the table. "She's learning to live with these new limitations. In a way, it feels like your body has betrayed you." Matty shook his head and exhaled. "The adjustment is probably harder on the ego than on the body."

As Matty continued, Jack considered his words. He ran his

hand over his jaw. Despite his cousin's lighthearted persona, Matty sometimes revealed a more serious side, a deeper one than people would expect if they didn't look beyond the jokes. The incident with the IED that had killed his K9 and wounded him had likely instigated that, forcing him to grow up in a flash.

Their server returned with their drinks. Matty took a sip of his beer.

Jack ran his hand over the condensation of the glass. "So what do I do?"

"Follow her lead. Be supportive in a way that seems right to her. *Not* to you." Matty motioned at Jack. "You have that big brother thing like Angelo, always trying to take care of people. Some people don't want to be taken care of."

Right. That was what Carrie had pointed out. Jack thought he knew what was best for people and didn't understand when they pushed back.

"Good advice. Thanks, man." Jack took a sip of his cold beer, and the tang lingered on his tongue.

"If it works out with Vivi, bring her down to Newport. The four of us can go out and do something together."

"I like your optimism, Matty." Jack grunted. "First, I need to see if she even wants to talk to me again."

JACK SPENT THE NEXT DAY RUMINATING WHILE HE HELPED HIS mother with some small home repairs.

As the inkling of a plan took shape, he smiled with satisfaction. He knew one place where he could find her, and he had a contact on the inside.

Jack called Ryan at the cat shelter. After a quick intro, Jack admitted, "I screwed up with Vivi."

"What happened?" Ryan replied.

"I pushed her to try rock climbing again. It didn't turn out like I'd hoped. She got frustrated and left. Told me to leave her alone."

"Ah, I can see that. She doesn't like being pushed."

"I want to make it up to her somehow. That's what I wanted to talk to you about." Jack tapped a pen on the table. "When is her next shift?"

CHAPTER 12

VIVI

Vivi grabbed a pet brush and rubbed the cat hair off a tiered climbing structure with vigor. She'd just finished scooping some litter boxes, but the scent of freshly turned litter lingered and she scrunched her nose.

"What's going on, Vivi?" Ryan asked as he stepped into the main area with a half-empty water bowl for the cats who liked to visit the office. "It's Wednesday, not your scheduled shift. You're practically living here this week."

Ah, he caught that. She'd been coming in more frequently this week, seeking distractions to avoid going home to her apartment—alone.

"Oh, you know. School's stressing me out and all," she replied with a casual wave. "This is where I can decompress from life."

"School, eh?" He raised a doubtful brow before stepping into the gated enclosure with the cleaning supplies.

A flash of when Jack had stepped in there with her when

she'd given him a tour returned. She'd backed into his chest. His broad, muscular chest that she'd loved to trail her fingers over, dipping into the crevices down his cut abs...

She shoved that image aside and resumed brushing away the fur with more force than necessary. "Sure. Spending a couple of hours with cats is better than meditating. Not as boring either."

Ryan turned on the faucet and filled the bowl. "You sure it has nothing to do with Jack?"

She paused and ground her teeth at hearing his name. Ryan had called her out, seeing through her flimsy excuses.

It didn't help her goal of distraction. It was already difficult enough to ignore all the visual cues that reminded her of the times she'd spent with Jack at the shelter. The near kiss here inside, the actual kiss outside, and that cat, Stella, sauntering about. She reminded Vivi of how adorable he'd looked when he kneeled down and let her crawl all over his lap, rubbing her chin and making her purr with pleasure.

He'd damn well made Vivi purr with pleasure, too.

She exhaled with a sigh. "Not sure what you're talking about, Ryan. I barely know the guy."

Ryan coughed while uttering, "Bullshit." His sandy-brown hair, longer in the front, fell over his face, and he brushed it back.

"It's true," she protested and resumed brushing at cat hair. "I mean, how can I really know someone I only ran into just over two weeks ago?"

Ryan stepped out of the cleaning area with the bowl of fresh water. "And spent plenty of time with since then. With how close you seemed to be, I'd have sworn you were a couple."

"Well, whatever it was we were doing, it's over now." She pulled a clump of fur off the brush and tossed it into a covered trash pail.

Ryan put the bowl of water down on a nearby table and pointed to his chest. "Tell Daddy all about it."

JACK

She reached for a nearby rag and tossed it at him. "I'm not going to call you that."

He caught the rag and put it beside the water bowl. "Vivi, stop stalling. Spill."

"Ugh, what do you want me to say? That I'm screwed up?" She threw her hands in the air.

"Screwed up, no." Ryan shook his head. "Too proud, yes." He gave her a single nod with a knowing glance.

She pursed her lips and turned away. It was an accurate assessment, one of her many faults, and she didn't appreciate the reminder. "I can't help that. It's the way I am."

"Pride is overrated. I don't think taking it down a notch is going to kill you," Ryan pointed out. "Especially if it helps you be happy."

During that short time with Jack, she was happy. *They* were happy. Until she'd let her hang-ups interfere.

While she assessed his words, Ryan added, "I'd never seen you light up like that, the way you did when you were around Jack. I dare say you had a pep in your step."

"That's the limp." She gave him a deadpan look.

He took two steps closer and squeezed her shoulder. "It was a *peppy* limp."

"It doesn't matter now," she replied with a dismissive wave. "He has a great job offer in DC. He should move there and find someone who can do all the things that make him happy."

"Like what?"

Vivi crossed her arms. "You are quite nosy, aren't you?"

"Of course." Ryan's wide grin turned Cheshire-like. "This is the first glimpse I've had with any part of your love life. Damn straight, I'm going to poke the bear until I get all the juicy details." He poked her upper arm twice, stepping back in between like a boxer light on his feet.

She brushed her hand away and tried not to laugh, but failed. "All right, fine." She plopped down on a red velvet loveseat that an old woman had donated, which the cats loved as evidenced by the fur Vivi often brushed. "So when we were stationed in Okinawa, we'd meet up at a rock climbing gym. I hadn't tried it since I'd been injured. He convinced me to go and give it a try."

Stella strolled over and jumped on the loveseat, curling up next to Vivi. It figured. Who would stroll over next to remind Vivi of what she'd lost? She stroked Stella's back, soft fur brushing her finger tips. Stella nudged Vivi's hand, so she rubbed her head and cheeks the way that Jack had done, giving her the affection she'd craved. Stella purred in appreciation.

Ryan leaned against the gated enclosure and prodded, "And?"

"It didn't go so well. My leg acted up." Vivi kept her hands busy with being attentive to Stella. "Figures it rained later that night. When I faced all those imposing walls, it felt like they were closing in on me. I freaked out and left. I used to look forward to that challenge, pushing myself with more difficult climbs. Now I don't even know if I could even support myself on the easiest bouldering wall that even little kids can whip across."

"Have you talked to him since?" Ryan asked.

"He's called, but I told him it wouldn't work between us. He's athletic and is better off finding someone better suited to his lifestyle. And he can pursue job opportunities wherever he likes." She gestured with a wide wave.

Ryan shook his head, clucking his tongue. "You are a stubborn fool, my dear."

"You don't know what it was like." Vivi squirmed in the loveseat. "I don't want people staring at me with pity when I'm struggling to do something that used to be so easy."

He pointed at her. "Ah, you and your pride again..."

She scowled. "I don't like feeling vulnerable like that."

"Let me get this straight." Ryan stepped away from the gate and stroked his beard while he paced before her. "This guy takes you out to do something you like to do—and because you got frustrated, you dumped his sorry ass?"

Coming from Ryan, it did make her sound rather petty.

"You're simplifying it. It's part of a bigger picture, Ryan. This is only one thing." She raised her index finger. "What about the job offer? He doesn't need to consider someone he's only been with for a blip of time as a factor when choosing his best options."

Ryan cocked his head and fixed a pointed stare on her. "Isn't he able to decide for himself?"

"Of course, but what about all the other things he wants to try?" She could hear the defensiveness in her tone. "He's super active and outdoorsy. I'm not able to do any of that anymore. At least, not in the same way."

"Enough with the pity party, sunshine." He wagged his finger. "You were once a bad ass, and you'll always be a bad ass." Ryan's expression turned sassy.

Her nostrils flared. She gave a frustrated wave. "What are you saying, Ryan? That I should go and make a fool out of myself in front of an audience? Maybe give them a front row seat to an anxiety attack."

He shrugged. "A fool who takes chances may lead a richer life than a queen with too much pride, sitting on her throne and watching the world go by."

She snorted. "Where did you get that from—a fortune cookie?"

"Maybe. It's true, though."

She blinked slowly, considering his words. Could Ryan be right? Was she letting her pride get in the way?

Yes.

The truth seeped in through a crack in her thick, stubborn skull.

She straightened her spine and met Ryan's gaze. "You're right. It's time for me to woman up."

She couldn't spend the rest of her days brooding about things she couldn't change. What was the point of dwelling on it? She'd felt sorry for herself long enough, and guilty about—too much. She owed it to those who didn't make it home to live her life. She'd been knocked down, but she was a fighter, and it was time to step back into the ring.

Or in this case, the rock climbing arena.

Ryan replied with a proud nod. "What do you plan to do?"

Her heartbeat ticked up a notch. "Stop hiding from my fears and face them. Learn to adjust to my life now and not compare it to the past."

"That's a great plan, Vivi." He grinned. "I'm rooting for you."

She took a deep breath as she pictured the next step. It might be tough, it might be frustrating, but she wouldn't know without trying. It was time to move beyond the comforting confines of the cat shelter, surrounded only by her furry, four-legged friends.

Too much damn pride had kept her from accepting she could still do the things she enjoyed. She just had to modify them.

"I'm rooting for you, cupcake," Ryan said.

Vivi smirked, remembering their earlier exchange. "You're the only one who gets to call me that."

She left the cat shelter twenty minutes later, resolved to move on—even if it meant pushing herself ahead one uneven step at a time.

JACK

After breakfast on Thursday morning, Jack stopped by a florist to pick up some flowers. He'd confirmed Vivi's next shift with Ryan. Jack meandered around the store, surrounding by the various floral scents.

White roses, that was perfect—a sign of his humility and surrender.

When he arrived at the cat shelter, he searched for her, ready to offer up the roses in surrender.

No sign of her in the main area or outside. Stella, the black cat, sauntered up to him, rubbing against his leg.

"Do you remember me, sweet girl?" He kneeled and rubbed her chin. Once she had a little affection, she rubbed against him for more. He grinned to himself. At least someone appreciated his efforts.

He walked into the office and greeted Ryan, who sat before the computer on his desk.

"Are those for me?" Ryan teased and reached for them. "You shouldn't have, but I'm glad you did."

Jack pulled them back. "Where's Vivi? I thought you said she'd be here."

Ryan exhaled and slumped his shoulders. "She called and said she'd be in later this morning. She didn't say why."

Jack lowered the flowers, buds down. Damn, he was such an idiot, standing there like a fool.

Ryan motioned to a worn brown chair opposite his desk. "Feel free to hang out and wait. Or wander around."

With all the tension that had built up inside Jack on anticipating seeing Vivi soon, he wouldn't be able to sit still. He glanced at a stack of adoption papers on Ryan's desk.

"What do you need from someone who wants to adopt a cat?" While he was here, he might as well make the most of it. He was moving forward with his new life as a civilian, but he liked the idea of a companion in the uncertainty ahead.

Ryan's eyes sparkled. "Are you interested? Or you know someone?"

Jack shrugged. "Stella and I seem to be hitting it off."

"She has quite the personality. Difficult to resist her charms."

The knowing lilt in Ryan's tone made Jack wonder if he was talking purely about Stella.

He furrowed his brows. "What do you need?"

Ryan leaned back in his desk chair. "We need to make sure it's a suitable match. Things we check on include the living situation. If you rent, we'll need confirmation that the landlord is okay with cats. We check with references to ensure you're a good candidate. If you've had cats in the past, we'll want to see some health records or check with the vet to see if you've taken cats for their routine check-ups and shots. If you have other pets, we'll discuss how they've reacted to other animals in the past. Since I know your family has plenty of experience, we can skip the reference checks." Ryan leaned forward. "But what's your living situation like?"

"I'm with my mom and sister. But I'm looking to buy a place of my own. It's my next step after I find a job."

Ryan raised his brows with a speculative look. "Around here?"

"Yes. You look surprised."

"I heard you might be moving to DC."

Jack grunted. "Vivi told you about that?"

"Perhaps."

"And?"

"That's all I'm going to say about that." Ryan made a zipping motion over his mouth. He glanced at a blank application on his desk. "Would you be around to take care of Stella?"

"I'm going into education, but nothing that should require late nights or long trips away from home."

Ryan's eyes twinkled with amusement. "If you're ready, I know which of our volunteers should interview you."

When Vivi entered the main area of the cat shelter a half an hour later wearing a bright orange volunteer shirt and her hair pulled into a messy bun, Jack stopped brushing the gray tabby with a mat forming on her belly and stood. His heart pounded like the rapid fire of a machine gun.

She froze and her eyes widened. "Jack, what are you doing here?"

A cat wandered up to her and brushed against her leg.

He rolled on the balls of his feet and then pointed to the white roses he'd left outside of the gated enclosure. Cats and roses could be a disaster.

Cats and roses—could be a band name.

Focus... stop being nervous and get in the game.

"I brought you some flowers to apologize and live up to my promise."

She blinked in rapid succession. "What promise?"

"I told you if you came to the rock climbing gym, I'd cover the poop scooping duties during your next shift. I'm a little late, but here to honor my word."

She peered at him with incredulity. "I didn't live up to my end of the bargain, considering I bolted." Lowering her gaze, she added, "In a rather dramatic departure."

"Hey, I didn't specify the terms. I said you had to go, *not* that you had to climb."

Her lips curled upwards. "You'd be a shitty lawyer."

"Tell me about it." He ran his fingers through his hair. "Listen, Viv, I'm sorry for pushing you. I get that I was out of line."

She glanced across the room. "No, you were right. Ryan's right, too—I'm too stubborn and proud. You had my best interests in mind, and I lashed out at you in frustration. It wasn't you I was mad at, it was me. The anxiety pushed me to panic and want to escape." She pinched the bridge of her nose. "It was yet another reminder of what I couldn't do anymore. I was angry at what had happened and overwhelmed facing what things are like now."

Jack placed his hand on his heart. "Still, I pushed you before you were ready."

"I *needed* that push."

Their eyes locked for a moment of silent understanding, and something more. A connection he'd never experienced with someone else. She was the one for him. Although many parts of his life were still in flux, his feelings for her were a certainty.

He swallowed. "You were brave to step in there. I am the one who has been a coward."

She cocked her head as she gazed at him. "How so?"

"You've confided in me, but I've been too chicken shit to do the same with you."

She shifted her stance. "About what?"

He eyed her carefully before responding. This was a conversation he wouldn't have with most people. Certain things he kept to himself. But this was Vivi—and she'd gone through so much herself. He drew in a long breath before replying.

He glanced at the red velvet loveseat where a gray cat curled up. "Can we sit?"

"Sure."

She sat beside the gray cat, who then scooted away. "Sorry, Cassidy," she said to the cat who found another spot on a cat climber.

He took the seat recently vacated by the cat, not caring if he ended up covered in fur. He took a deep breath and exhaled before raising his eyes to meet hers. "I told you that my dad died when I was twelve. I've been thinking about him a lot since I've been home."

"That makes sense with being back with your family." Her voice sounded soothing, encouraging him to continue.

"What I've been thinking about how I've been following in his footsteps since he died." His ribs felt tight. "Before I deployed to Okinawa, I had a tour in Kabul. I lost one of my Marines in a firefight. He was shot right in the chest. We—we couldn't save him." Jack blew out another breath. "Martin was only twenty-three. He was someone's son. A husband. And a father of an infant who would never know his father." Tension twisted his muscles through a meat grinder.

"Oh Jack, I'm sorry." Her tone was gentle. Genuine.

He counted to seven before continuing. "I've always felt responsible. Logically, I know there's nothing I could have done to change things, since you can't rewrite the past." He lowered his gaze to the loveseat and rubbed the velvet beneath his fingers. "I think of all the things that could have gone differently, if only I'd changed one tiny factor that wouldn't have put him in that spot where the bullet pierced his chest at that particular moment." Shame and regret twisted him into knots. "Knowing that he left a family behind eats away at me. It's similar to what happened with my father." He swallowed a lump in his throat. "My family."

Vivi gasped. "That must be tough." She placed her hand on his thigh. "What you went through..."

He glanced at her hand and then raised his eyes to meet hers. Hers were full of warmth and compassion.

"It finally became clear to me why the military wasn't the right path ahead. I don't want to make the calls that could jeopardize someone's life or tear—tear apart a family." His breath came quicker as he searched her eyes. "An officer like me could make a call that leads to a lifelong consequence—or worse—for someone like you."

Vivi released an audible exhale. "That's an incredible amount of pressure and responsibility." After two more pounding heartbeats, she added, "I'm glad you told me."

So was he. Finally, he was able to wrestle those fragments and flashes of feelings into something that made sense in his head. She'd encouraged him to face those fears and uncertainties, no matter how painful they were.

She kept her hand on his leg, a silent promise that she was

there for him. "I know it's difficult to put those intense emotions into words."

Vivi didn't have to say anything else. Her presence comforted him.

She understood.

"Survivor's guilt is a bitch-and-a-half, isn't it?" He forced a grin.

"Sure is." She raised her brows and nodded.

He put his hand on hers. "Enough of that. I came here with a promise to help out, not sit around on my ass. What do you want me to do first?" He rose to his feet.

She stood beside him. "You really want to help out?"

"Of course. I'm sure Cassidy will appreciate me freeing up her seat."

"You're probably right." Vivi glanced over at Cassidy, still staring at him as if indeed ready to reclaim her seat.

When Vivi turned back to Jack, she beamed. Her smile branded him with her happiness. He'd never forget that look.

"Come on." She pointed to the back. "There are a few cat carriers out back that someone donated, which need to be cleaned."

He spent the next hour or so helping Vivi with her routine, which included the poop scooping duties he'd agreed to. It felt good to do something with his hands after the emotional weight he'd unloaded.

After they washed up, she asked, "Are you free after this?"

"Yes, why?"

"I'm wondering if you'd go back to the rock climbing gym with me."

So many thoughts raced through his head. Did this mean she was ready to give it another shot? "Are you serious?"

"Yes." Her eyes shined bright with determination. "That's where I was before I came here."

He replayed her words in his head, not sure if he'd heard them correctly.

"Once Ryan talked some sense into me, I reconsidered my stance. I remember you telling me about your cousin, and I watched videos of vets and heard their stories. Some had lost a leg and learned how to climb with adaptive equipment. Who am I to shove the idea aside, thinking *I can't?* If they were up for the challenge, having more obstacles to overcome, then I can do it. They inspired me to take a chance and push myself."

"That's wonderful, Viv."

An orange tabby wandered over, and Vivi crouched to pet it. "This morning, I went back to that rock climbing gym and talked to a trainer about options. I need to take it slow, start with easy climbs, but I took the first step—always the hardest, right?" She grinned and stood.

"Right," he agreed.

"It was tough to adjust to my body's limitations." Her smile vanished. "I thought everyone was staring at me thinking *oh, look at that poor girl.* It was easy to get frustrated, and I was ready to give up, but I thought of you, with that look on your face, believing in me even when I didn't believe in myself." She angled her head and gazed at him with appreciation. "And I gritted my teeth and tried again. After a while, I stopped worrying about what others thought of me and began to enjoy the process. Eventually, I did it." She shrugged. "Sure, it was the easiest part of the gym in the bouldering area, but I was off the ground." Her eyes gleamed. "It was exhilarating to push myself again, getting lost in that mental space when you climb. Know what I mean?"

"I do." He stared at her, and his heartbeat raced. "I admire you."

Her brows furrowed and she her gaze dropped. "One thing that bothers me is that I can't keep up with you. I might never be able to do so."

That's what she was upset about? It wasn't even an issue. "Don't be," he reassured her. "I've spent years competing, facing challenges, and breaking personal records. With you, it's different. It's not a competition, it's an experience. And I'd enjoy any kind of experiences with you—from going to dinner or watching a movie," he admitted. "It doesn't have to be some race."

"What about DC?"

He shook his head and motioned decisively with his hands. "Off the table."

"Why?" She searched his eyes.

"I like my options here more." He stepped closer to Vivi and cupped her chin.

Her eyes glistened. "Me, too."

His voice caught somewhere in his throat, and he swallowed. "You told me you didn't want people to notice you're different. But the thing is, to me, you are. Different in a wonderful way." His breath came quicker now and skin turned hot. He moved his hand up and stroked her cheek. "You're not only beautiful, but unique. And I wouldn't want you any other way. I'll never forget the moment you entered my classroom years ago, changing my life for the better."

Her lips quivered, eyes glistened, and then she broke into a smile. "If I hadn't been hurt, who knows where I'd be stationed right now. One silver lining to my injury is that it gave me a chance to find and be with you."

In that moment, his senses fired up as all the uncertainties in his life disappeared. He was falling in love with her. He guessed he had been for some time, as no woman had compared to her since they'd met. And now in the face of her adversity, her courage, determination, and tenacity made him admire her even more. "You're amazing."

"Oh stop," she said with a wave as her cheeks turned pink. "So many others take on this challenge without all the doubts I

JACK

had. I want to go back to try climbing with you. Will you be my partner?"

"In more ways than one, I hope."

Her gaze met his, and heat simmered between them, shooting bolts of awareness all through his body. She excited him in so many ways. Their connection was underlined with something else—a silent sort of understanding that they were both committed to making it work.

Vivi nodded. "In more ways than one."

His entire body lightened with vibrancy. Only she could do that to him. "You seem to have been a proper kick in the ass for me, as well. Besides confronting my demons, I've been busy trying to take the next step in my life."

"You have?"

"Yes, with teaching. You reminded me what I love about teaching—when I'm able to reach someone with that passion. That's what I want to do—inspire people. You challenged me to take a risk."

She blinked twice. "How did I manage that?" Her brows drew closer in question.

"By encouraging me to dig deeper and figure out what I want. I learned it was time to break away from living my father's life and to start living my own. I sent resumes and talked to people. My mom always knows someone who knows someone. She thought of a teacher who volunteers here at the shelter on Saturdays. She works in the Boston Public Schools and got me in touch with a director for a new program to reach a difficult student population. Turns out he served in the Marines and that made me stand out among the candidates. When we met, he said my military experience would be an asset, all the structure and discipline is key. I never considered teaching at a high school before, but I'm excited about the opportunity. I'll need to take more classes, but that's fine. I like to learn."

"We're talking a tough group in an inner city school?" Her brows arched. "Sounds challenging."

"Says someone who's been deployed to a war zone." He grinned.

She shook her head. "I don't have it in me to deal with a class of high school students. But you do. If anyone can reach them, it's you. Your patience, your passion, even your bizarre sense of humor with those dreadful puns—you'd be great at it, Jack. I'm thrilled for you."

He glowed under her compliment. She'd helped bring out the potential in him, and it sounded like he had somewhat of a positive effect on her. His insides softened, practically turned to mush.

Vivi rubbed her hands together. "Enough talking, it's time to act."

"How so?"

"That quick visit this morning might have given me the bug again." She gave him a brilliant smile. "Let's climb."

CHAPTER 13

VIVI

When Vivi entered the rock climbing gym, the upbeat music pumped into her veins. She was eager to take on this new challenge. How different from the last time she'd been there with Jack. The walls with climbers didn't appear as daunting. The scent of chalk reminded something she'd once enjoyed a great deal—even more so with Jack.

When he'd arrived at the cat shelter earlier with white roses, her heart had pitter-pattered like raindrops on a tin roof. Her outlook had brightened even more so throughout the day. She couldn't think of a more perfect day spending it doing the things she loved with the man she—well—had probably fallen in love with long ago.

Everyone was fighting some battle, even if it wasn't visible. Even someone who appeared so confident and put together like Jack. He confided in her and that meant a lot. It meant everything.

Maybe they could deal with their demons together.

She was learning to accept that things had changed, and she had to learn to live with it to move on. Sure, she couldn't handle the tough climbs she had loved, but she was back in the gym again, with a man once so out of reach. If the impossible could come to fruition in one part of her life, maybe she could break through other limitations as well.

"Where would you like to start?" Jack asked.

His eyes shone with more green today than blue. Beautiful eyes that gazed at her, only her. The lighter streaks in his hair contrasted with the black on his shirt, which clung to his fit upper body with delicious perfection. She was one lucky woman.

"Bouldering."

One song ended and the next one began—*Conquest* by the White Stripes. She reached for the first grip, shifting her weight. She couldn't support her full weight on her injured leg, but if she used the wider grips and shifted much of her weight to other limbs, she could manage.

It was a workout, although it didn't have the adrenaline-pumping rush of a vertical climb.

"Let's try one of these walls," Jack said. He pointed to the easiest challenges marked by lower numbers. "I'll belay you."

Instinct almost led her to decline, say she wasn't ready. Instead, she took a deep breath. After she exhaled, she said, "Okay."

After she put on the equipment, and he tied her to him, she took the first step off the ground.

The climb was more difficult than she'd remembered, and she stumbled. After a few more stuttering starts, she was ready to call it quits.

"You've got this, Viv," Jack encouraged. "Go as slow as you need. Keep going."

Taking a few deep breaths to get beyond the frustration, she listened to the surrounding sounds. Imagine Dragons' *Natural* pumped through the speakers. Someone had fun with the playlists, which was something she could appreciate.

She reopened her eyes, ignored what the other climbers were doing, and then focused on her path up. It took several more attempts before she moved past the awkwardness with her new physical challenges.

With practice, she made progress and was able to climb part of the route. Such a small accomplishment gave her a tremendous rush.

After Jack lowered her to the ground, she threw her arms around him. "That felt incredible."

"You did awesome." He beamed at her with a proud expression.

She pulled back and gazed up at him. "Looks like all I needed was for you to get me off my stubborn, sorry ass."

He laughed.

"What's so funny?"

"I would describe it as a perfectly fine, sexy ass that I desperately wanted to touch while watching you climb up the wall." He slid his hands down her back.

She slipped out of his grip before he reached her butt and raised an index finger. "You better keep your hands on the rope and not my ass while you're belaying me." With a sly smile, she added, "But later tonight is a different story."

His eyes gleamed with excitement. "Can't wait."

He reached out and stroked her arm. Something else shimmered in eyes. Admiration?

"I've always known you were determined, Vivi, but I've never been more impressed than seeing you climb that wall today."

A pleasant warmth filled her. "I wouldn't have done it without you."

He nodded and groaned. "I know, I pushed you. I'm learning to back off."

"No, you believed in me," she clarified. "Most people give me a pitying look, reminding me of what I've lost. You encouraged me to try something I once loved."

She stared at the wall. Although she wanted to support Jack and then go for another round herself, her limbs were heavy from the new activity. "Hope you don't mind, but that tired me out. I need a break."

"Go for it. I'll get a couple of climbs in. I'm sure I can find someone to belay me."

That was a relief. She wasn't sure she could do it, which would take stability to ground herself on two feet to support him. One step at a time.

She got an iced tea from a vending machine and sat on a worn brown sofa in the seating area. Fall Out Boy's *Centuries* played. She adjusted her position to be able to watch him climb.

He chose a route moderate in difficulty. A guy belayed him and Jack ascended up the walls with finesse. His muscles were defined as he pulled himself up and his face burned with determination. She took a large sip. He was captivating, and she couldn't keep her eyes off him.

Picturing spending the night with him again made her flush. Her skin tingled with a slow rising. She'd never yearned for anyone as she had for Jack. And now that she'd swallowed some of her damn pride, they actually had a chance to start something.

Plus, he got her back in here. Her training in the gym would take practice, like it had taken time with physical therapy.

Her future appeared much brighter with Jack in it. Already she'd danced and climbed, both because of his encouragement. Maybe she'd take on new challenges as well.

Could she do something for him? A light sensation fluttered inside. Perhaps she had already, encouraging him to teach.

A relationship was one of the biggest challenges of all. And she was looking forward to building one with Jack. Apart they lacked something in their lives, but somehow together they worked.

After Vivi finished up with some physical therapy exercises and stretching on a worn blue exercise mat, Jack strode over and joined her. He stretched beside her and she couldn't resist staring at how his muscles shifted beneath his skin.

After a few minutes, he asked, "Ready to get out of here?"

"Yes." She stood and walked over to the locker where she'd stashed her belongings.

"How about we pick up some groceries, and I'll cook at my place? My mom and Carrie are antique shopping in Western Mass, which means I have the house to myself."

She turned to him. "You cook?"

"Apparently, my shrimp scampi is edible." He flashed a boyish grin. "I think my chicken marsala is decent too, if you're brave enough to try it."

She replied with a suggestive smile. "You know I love a challenge as much as you do."

"Great, let's go."

"I'm all sweaty," she said. "I should stop by my place to take a quick shower."

"Or you can shower at my place." His mock innocent expression shifted into a devilish one.

"Flowers, food, a hot shower—this day is looking up." She picked up the gear she'd rented and dropped them at the front desk.

He followed with his and they walked out the exit.

The sun had started to set, casting streaks of orange and purple overhead.

"Soon, I hope to have my own place, so we don't have to work around my family's schedule. I'm checking out a couple of open houses this weekend."

Vivi arched her brows. "Buying?"

"Yes. I don't want to rent. I'm ready to put down some solid roots around here." He spread one arm before them and then turned back to her. "Vivi, I want to talk to you about something."

She shrugged. "Go for it."

"I've been thinking about making a commitment to this female." His tone turned serious. "But I'm not sure I'm ready to take the next step."

How he was going about it was odd, but whatever. "We don't have to rush into anything, Jack. We can take it slow."

"I'm not talking about us."

Her gut tightened, the ground seemed unsteady. She fought to keep her voice level, but each word came out slow and frosty. "What are you talking about, Jack?""

"A commitment. It's scary, but maybe everyone feels that way."

Her breath came quick. Invisible daggers pierced her insides. Just when she thought everything was going so well with the two of them, that they might really have a chance…

"You know her quite well," Jack added. "In fact, you introduced me to her."

How could he be so nonchalant about it? He even had a small smile tugging at the corner of his mouth. Her blood filled with venom as she scrambled to keep up. Who the hell had she introduced him to?

"I have *no* idea who you're talking about," she said through gritted teeth.

"Sure you do. She has stunning green eyes." He nodded toward Vivi. "You pointed them out yourself."

Her self-control faltered. "Jack, stop playing with me. If you've been stringing me along all this time, I swear I'm going to freak out!"

"All right, all right." He cocked his head and grinned. "You're cute when you're angry, by the way."

"I'm not angry." She crossed her arms, huffing through her nose. "Who is it?"

They walked by a park. One section was enclosed as a dog park and several ran across the grounds.

"Stella."

"Stella? Who the hell's that?" She turned to face Jack.

"Pretty black cat. Green eyes." He raised a brow. "Anyone tell you that you swear like a sailor when you're mad?"

Vivi blinked several times as she pulled the pieces together. "Oh!" She swatted him on the arm. "Why would you mess with me that way? Dick move, Conroy."

"I don't know. It all sort of came out as I started to tell you. Maybe I needed something light to counter all the heavy emotional tension I've dealt with today." He shrugged. "Or maybe I wanted to see how you'd react." He cocked his head and arched a brow. "You're super cute when you're jealous—or should I say *catty*."

She suppressed a smile. "I'm going to kill you, Jack Conroy! This is worse than that pathetic attempt at a UFO story!"

"Funny, how you didn't fall for that or Bigfoot, yet you think I could be interested in another woman?" he teased. "Impossible, Vivi. You're the one." He caressed her cheek.

Her heart fluttered, but she wouldn't let him off that easy. "You're still a dead man."

He sighed. "That's tragic timing for Stella. Just when there was talk about adoption…"

Her frustration dissipated with hope for one of the beloved shelter cats. "What? Are you serious?

They reached his truck. He guided her backwards, so she leaned against it, and then he put his arms around both sides as he gazed at her. "That depends. I already talked to Ryan, but I want to talk it over with you."

A faint scent of perspiration from their workout lingered on him. It wasn't at all unpleasant. "About what exactly?"

Jack peered down at her with an amused expression. "He assigned you to interview me."

"Did he now?" Vivi raised one brow. "Ryan seems to be taking quite an interest when it comes to getting the two of us to work together."

"He's a born matchmaker." Jack raised one hand. "People with cats." He raised the other. "People with people."

Vivi planted her hands on her hips. It was time for payback. "Are you ready for your interview now?"

"You already know what you need. I have experience taking care of cats, yada yada…"

"Oh no, no, no." She waved her finger. "You don't get off easy just because you've slept with me. *Especially* after what you just put me through."

Jack furrowed his brows. "What does that mean?"

"It means start by filling out an application. I want references." She clapped one hand into the other. "A full list of pets you've owned."

"What? Are you kidding me?"

She gave him a dead-on stare. "Do I look like I'm playing around? I need to know if you'd be a good match."

Jack grabbed her by the waist, pulling her toward him. Their faces were only inches apart. "You know we would be perfect together."

Her pulse quickened. Having him so near left her instantly breathless. "Are we still talking about you and Stella?"

"Maybe." He lowered his head, moving his lips tantalizingly close. "And maybe we're talking about you and me."

He kissed her, gently at first, but as the kiss deepened, sparks ignited with growing desire. When they pulled away from each other, she was panting.

"You make one hell of an argument." She gave him a one-sided grin. "Maybe you wouldn't be so shitty at law after all."

EPILOGUE

VIVI

Vivi took his father's arm after the opening notes of Mendelssohn's Wedding March signaled it was time. He led her down the path in the courtyard of the Boston Public Library. Surrounded by white marble arches in a Roman-designed plaza, they walked past the fountain and a bronze statue in the center of the pool.

She wore white flats beneath her wedding gown, a simple yet elegant silk dress with thin white shoulder straps. The satin fabric swooshed around her legs, reminding her of the way the blue satin one had done the night she ran into Jack at the cat shelter gala. Her life had changed so much since then.

Jack had started his new position in the Boston schools, and she finished out the school semester. She'd picked up a part-time job at a local pet hospital while continuing to volunteer at the cat shelter.

And thanks to him, she'd learned to love rock climbing again. They'd even gone a couple of times with his cousin,

Matty, and his wife, Jenna, who lived down in Newport. Matty had a great sense of humor dealing with his own injury, which helped her lighten up about hers. The four of them had talked about going on a ski trip in the White Mountains next month. Matty's brother, Angelo, and his wife, Catherine, would also try to make it. Vivi wasn't sure her legs would be able to bear the pressure of downhill skiing, but knowing they had adaptive skiing gear gave her more options.

Jack had proposed on the Fourth of July with one of his corniest lines yet, but one she'd treasure forever. He'd pointed toward the fireworks exploding overhead and had said, "This is how I feel inside whenever I'm around you." He then lowered himself to one knee and proposed, "Vivi, will you marry me."

Of course, she'd said yes.

They'd planned this intimate wedding in early January before she resumed college classes. Tomorrow, they'd escape the New England winter for a week in the Caribbean.

Now she approached the man she loved, surrounded by their closest family and friends. Her breath caught in her throat. He was devastatingly dashing standing in a tux at the end of the courtyard. She caught his eyes and her heart fluttered with unprecedented joy.

The next chapter in their life together was about to begin.

JACK

Dreams could come true.

How else could Jack explain the woman of his dreams headed toward him, looking more beautiful than ever in a white silk gown?

Was she really willing to commit to him for life?

His palms turned hot. A few years ago, continents away, he never thought this could be possible. Maybe when it came to love, some obstacles weren't impossible after all. It all came down to timing and second chances.

He had a second chance with Vivi and he'd spend the rest of his life trying to prove to her that it was worth it.

They were building their lives together step by step. They'd bought a fixer-upper, which not only housed Stella, the black cat, but two others. His sister teased how he was becoming a crazy cat person himself. He couldn't deny how much he loved Stella. She often followed him from room to room or curled up near him on the couch and purred.

On the weekends, he worked on the house, something he'd remember his father doing when he was young. Jack's job working with kids in the inner city was tough, but he loved it.

Vivi was less than ten feet away now. His heart thundered in his ears. Was this just a dream, and he'd wake up alone, aching, yearning—wondering where a woman he'd met on another continent had ended up in the world?

Her father kissed her cheek and handed her over to Jack. He took her hand. The warm vibe soothed him, convincing him that this was real.

Vivi gave him a brilliant smile and his insides melted. He stared into the eyes of his soon-to-be wife and swallowed.

Yes, this moment was real. No dream could ever make him feel so alive.

***

A NOTE FROM THE AUTHOR:

I hope you enjoyed Vivi and Jack's romance. Their background was inspired by when I'd served over in the Marines in Okinawa. Like many writers, I observed and thought what if...

A few years ago, my daughter and I volunteered at a cat shelter, where we adopted our two crazy kittens. After we volunteered at the fundraising gala, I had the perfect setting for Jack and Vivi's reunion.

We're going to head on over to the other side of the world to Okinawa, Japan, the next book in this series— where Vince and Emma (from Vince) are deployed. Read more about the friends to lovers, marriage-of-convenience romance in Slade!

Like Jack's story, Slade was inspired by my time deployed over in Okinawa.

WANT MORE NAVY SEALs AND MARINES? JOIN ME AT PATREON TO go behind the scenes with exclusive content, bonus scenes and stories from the Anchor Me series, and signed books.

https://www.patreon.com/lisacarlisle

~ Lisa

JOIN MY VIP READERS LIST!

Don't miss any new releases, giveaways, specials, or freebies! Access exclusive bonus content.

Join the VIP list and you'll receive a welcome gift, including free books!

www.lisacarlislebooks.com

I also have a Facebook Reader group.

Let's have some fun talking about books and fur babies!

https://www.facebook.com/groups/147725722605800

BOOK LIST

Visit LisaCarlisleBooks.com to learn more!

Anchor Me

Navy SEALs, Marines, and hometown heroes. Each one encounters his most complicated mission yet, when he will find a woman from his past—who changes his future.

- *Antonio (a novella available for free here)*
- *Angelo*
- *Vince*
- *Matty*
- *Jack*
- *Slade*
- *Mark*
- *Leo*

Night Eagle Operations

A paranormal romantic suspense novel

- *When Darkness Whispers*

Salem Supernaturals

Paranormal chick lit with comedy, romance, and mystery!

- *Rebel Spell*
- *Hot in Witch City*
- *Dancing with My Elf*
- *Night Wedding*
- *Bite Wedding*

- Sprite Wedding

White Mountain Shifters (A Wolf Shifter Trilogy)
Howls Romance

When three wolf shifters meet their fated mates at their ski resort, the forbidden attraction may spark a war.

- *The Reluctant Wolf and His Fated Mate*
- *The Wolf and His Forbidden Witch*
- *The Alpha and His Enemy Wolf*

The White Mountain Shifters series is connected to the Salem Supernaturals and Underground Encounters series.

Underground Encounters

Steamy paranormal romances set in an underground goth club that attracts vampires, witches, shifters, and gargoyles.

- *Book 0: CURSED (a gargoyle shifter story)*
- *Book 1: SMOLDER (a vampire / firefighter romance)*
- *Book 2: FIRE (a witch / firefighter romance)*
- *Book 3: IGNITE (a feline shifter / rock star romance)*
- *Book 4: BURN (a vampire / shapeshifter rock romance)*
- *Book 5: HEAT (a gargoyle shifter romance)*
- *Book 6: BLAZE (a gargoyle shifter rockstar romance)*
- *Book 7: COMBUST (vampire / witch romances)*
- *Book 8: INFLAME (a gargoyle shifter / witch romance)*
- *Book 9: TORCH (a gargoyle shifter / werewolf romance)*
- *Book 10: SCORCH (an incubus vs succubus demon romance)*

Stone Sentries Trilogy

Meet your perfect match the night of the super moon — or your perfect match for the night. A cop teams up with a gargoyle shifter when demons attack Boston.

- *Tempted by the Gargoyle*
- *Enticed by the Gargoyle*
- *Captivated by the Gargoyle*

Highland Gargoyles (A Complete Series)

When a witch sneaks into forbidden territory on a divided isle, she's caught by a shifter. One risk changes the fate for all…

- *Knights of Stone: Mason*
- *Knights of Stone: Lachlan*
- *Knights of Stone: Bryce*
- *Seth: a wolf shifter romance*
- *Knights of Stone: Calum*
- *Stone Cursed*
- *Knights of Stone: Gavin*

Chateau Seductions

An art colony on a remote New England island lures creative types—and supernatural characters. Steamy paranormal romances.

- *Darkness Rising*
- *Dark Velvet*
- *Dark Muse*
- *Dark Stranger*
- *Dark Pursuit*

Berkano Vampires

A shared author world with dystopian paranormal romances.

- *Immortal Resistance*

Blood Courtesans

A shared author world with the vampire blood courtesans.

- *Pursued: Mia*

Visit LisaCarlisleBooks.com to learn more!

ACKNOWLEDGMENTS

As always, I am tremendously grateful to everyone who helps make each book possible, helping me shape the strange ideas in my head into a coherent story. Huge thanks to my critique partners, editor, beta readers, proofreaders, ARC readers, Street Team, and you, the reader! Thank you for spending time with me in these worlds with characters I love.

ABOUT THE AUTHOR

USA Today bestselling author Lisa Carlisle loves stories with misfits or outcasts. Her romances have been named Top Picks at Night Owl Reviews and the Romance Reviews.

When she was younger, she worked in a variety of jobs, moving to various countries. She served in the military in Okinawa, Japan; backpacked alone through Europe; and worked in Paris before returning to the U.S. She owned a bookstore for a few years as she loves to read. She's now married to a fantastic man, and they have two kids and two crazy cats.

Visit her website at:
Lisacarlislebooks.com

Sign up for her newsletter to hear about new releases, specials, and freebies:
http://lisacarlislebooks.com/subscribe/

Lisa loves to connect with readers. You can find her on:

Facebook
  TikTok
  Instagram
  Pinterest
  Twitter
  Goodreads